FIRE

in the

HILLS

Also by Anna Myers

RED-DIRT JESSIE

ROSIE'S TIGER

GRAVEYARD GIRL

FIRE

in the

HILLS

Anna Myers

Walker and Company

NEW YORK

First published in the United States of America in 1996 by Walker
Publishing Company, Inc.

Published simultaneously in Canada by Thomas Allen & Son Canada,
Limited, Markham, Ontario

Library of Congress Cataloging-in-Publication Data
Myers, Anna.
Fire in the hills/Anna Myers.
p. cm.
Summary: After her mother's death, sixteen-year-old Hallie faces
changes in her life in the hills of eastern Oklahoma in 1918, as she
takes over caring for her family and begins thinking about life as a
woman.
ISBN 0-8027-8421-6 (hardcover)
[1. Family life—Oklahoma—Fiction. 2. Country life—Oklahoma—
Fiction. 3. Oklahoma—Fiction. 4. World War, 1939–1945—United
States—Fiction.] I. Title.
PZ7.M9814Fi 1996
[Fic]—dc20 95-39928
CIP AC
Book design by Jennifer Ann Daddio
Printed in the United States of America
2 4 6 8 10 9 7 5 3

To the memory of my father, Ross Hoover,
and of my mother, Cecil Eaton Hoover,
who also loved the mountain flowers.

TRADING FAVORS WITH PAW PAW

by Ben Myers

I remember you,
Oil Field Angel.

I remember the grease
and dust clinging to the rim
of my nose
in the sun cracked cab
of the old yellow Ford.
I remember the air
sagging with after-shave
in the barber shop
where we had my hair cut
for the first time.

I remember the moon
out in the thin gray of daytime
for your funeral,
plump as the silver dollars
you slipped me
from the potato sacks
of your baggy khaki pockets.

I remember carrying your casket
to be planted in the embrace
of the Oklahoma earth,
holding the rail of the coffin
was like holding your red mountain
    hand
for the last time.

MOUNTAIN FORK WOMAN

by Paul Myers

Mountain Fork Woman,
Secret as the stones
At the bottom of the creek,
Your eyes hold the seasons.
And the dreams are scattered
Through the tops of pines
Where the song-birds watched
The girl behind the mule
Singing
    Her
        Way
            Back
                Home . . . .

FIRE
in the
HILLS

1

THE ROSES IN THE OLD YARD were an easement to the girl Hallie, who kept her eyes on them. She knew, too, where wild violets grew between the rocks on the mountainside. She would gather a bouquet for her mother, who also found pleasure in them.

For her grave, jeered a voice from somewhere inside her, but the girl shook her head violently.

"I'll fetch you flowers tomorrow, Ma," she said to the white form on the bed. "Bunches of violets, and buttercups, and some mountain pink."

The woman stirred, but the fever-dried lips did not speak, had not spoken since the request to be moved. "I'd be pleased to be out," she had whispered, "to get a breath and hear the little ones playing."

"Fields need tending," Mason said after the move and, like silent players of follow the leader, his sons filed after him. Only Turner, nine years old, stopped to look back just once before disappearing into the pines.

With the baby clutched to her thin chest Hallie sat beside her mother's bed. "He don't need holding whilst he sleeps," her father had commented, but Starlin had carried out the old rocker and Hallie settled herself there, clutching the tiny body to her as if for warmth.

"Poor little mite," she said softly. "Poor little mite, a week old and no name for you."

It was a surprise to the girl, seeing that her mother's eyes were open. "Ma," she said, "should I cool your face with a cloth?"

"No." A thin hand rose slightly from the bed and gestured weakly toward the two children playing with rocks near the stoop. "You'll have to do for them, Hallie. It will be you as has to do for them."

"They don't need nothing, Ma. Let me do for you."

"It's later I'm meaning. You'll be needing a heart like that of a woman grown. Poor little Hallie. I hate such to settle on you, child, but there's no help for it."

"Let me bring you a bite, Ma. Baby will be wanting to eat. You got to have food." The girl was desperate to change the subject. Even the fevered moans were better.

"It's Mary Jones will be feeding my baby. Take him over there as soon as . . ." The woman paused, reaching out to stroke the girl's arm. "Sweet Hallie. You take him to Mary yourself. Now, Mary is rough and hard, but her young ones is always fat." The woman's eyes closed again.

"Ma," said the girl, trying not to scream. "Ma, you can't die."

"We all do, child. We all do. There is worst things. Sing to me, Hallie. It will rest us both."

The girl sat back in the chair, closed her eyes, and began

to sing, blocking out everything but the words. Her voice was strong and sweet and clear, like the water over the rocks of the Mountain Fork.

"There's a land that is fairer than day,
and by faith we can see it afar;
For the Father waits over the way
to prepare us a dwelling place there.
In the sweet by and by,
we shall meet on that beautiful shore;
In the sweet by and by,
we shall meet on that beautiful shore."

When the song was finished Hallie opened her eyes, knowing that her mother was dead.

"Burch," she called the little boy from his play, "you run to the field and tell Pa he will be obliged to stop work."

Hallie watched her father as he came to the bed and stood looking down at his wife. "Not many knows it, but your Pa feels things real deep," her mother had once told her. Remembering those words, the girl searched the man's face. "We'll put her at San Bois," Mason said. "Brack, you go see Erwart about getting the grave ready. Starlin, get the box started."

And so, thought Hallie, death is no different than cotton picking, just another reason to give orders to the boys.

But then Mason reached out to touch the limp dark hair

on the dead head. "Never did wear jewels, did you, Pearl? Never did."

His voice held no emotion, but Hallie, having heard the story from her mother, was touched. "Follow me and you'll wear jewels," Mason had told the young Pearl. Hallie had imagined the scene many times. Mason was a trail driver, strong and dark in the saddle. Pearl's face was full then and there was no sadness in her eyes as she stood at the town well, laughing up at the man on the horse. She had followed him, too, after he had searched the mountains for her home and had returned to court her. They had left the Ozarks of Arkansas, but Pearl had yearned for hills, and they had settled on this sloping farm where she bore nine children. The first two, twins, were buried in a fenced area behind the cabin.

The girl wanted to speak without crying. She never cried in front of her father. "Why you taking her to San Bois? If we was to bury her here, I could gather her flowers every day."

"No," said the man. "A proper cemetery is the place. Time will come we won't be here on this hill. Cattle ought not to be grazing on your ma's grave." Taking away his hand from his wife's hair, he turned to touch briefly the girl's identical tresses. Hallie could only vaguely remember ever before being touched by her father.

The baby in her arms stirred. "I needs to be taking him to Mary Jones," she said as she turned to walk away quickly, glad to let the tears flow down her cheeks. She was out of the yard and well down the trail toward the Joneses' place before she realized they were behind her. Turning, she observed them, Turner, Burch, and little Dovie, holding hands and huddled together, faces dirty from wiped tears.

"Come on," she said. "You can walk up here alongside me." They ran to her, relieved.

"Are you giving him to Mary Jones?" Burch asked, nodding his head in the baby's direction.

"No, sir. No sir! I most certainly am not!" said the girl. "I am asking Mary will she feed him with her young one for just a spell." She shifted the infant in her arms. "This here baby is a Horton, and I will tell you what we are going to do this very minute. We are going to name him."

"Our very own selves?" asked Dovie.

"Our very own selves," said the girl.

"What will we name him?" asked Turner.

"I don't know as yet, but we got to do it quick. I'll not be taking a Horton nameless to the Joneses' place. The good Lord only knows what they would stick on him for a name."

"We could call him Pearl," said Burch. "That's Ma's name."

"That's it," said the girl. "You said it right, almost." She shifted the baby, allowing a hand to pat the small boy's back. "We can't name him Pearl, him being a boy, but Pearly will do. I've heard tell of men named Pearly. This is Pearly M. Horton, and he belongs to us."

Mary Jones was on her porch, one bare foot on a rail. In her hand was a big butcher knife. She looked up only briefly from her toenail cutting. "Your ma's dead, I reckon."

"Yes, ma'am." Hallie kept her eyes on the toenail trimming.

"And you be wanting me to take in that youngun to feed." Mary looked up and motioned for Hallie to come closer. Then she put out her index finger and poked at the bundle in the girl's arms until it responded with a strong wail.

"Well, it's still alive at least," she said as if she had doubted the fact. "Bring any napkins?" Mary spat tobacco into an earthenware jar.

"I forgot," said the girl miserably.

"Well, never mind." Mary waved her arm at the yard, where white baby napkins hung on a line. "I've got plenty. Nice and white too, ain't they? I like things clean! Omer!" she yelled into the house. "I told you them rocks needs scrubbing."

A tall red-haired young man came out the side door with a bucket in his hands and headed for the huge boulders that marked the entrance to the Joneses' yard. Mary Jones prided herself on the fact that every rock was scrubbed white and the hard earth swept clean in her yard.

"She's clean all right, at least things around her, but I wouldn't drink her buttermilk. Not with that filthy spitting," Hallie remembered her ma saying. Now she was begging Mary Jones to feed her baby brother.

"Well," said Mary, "hand him here."

Hallie laid the baby in the woman's arms.

"Scrawny, ain't he?" said Mary between spits. "Don't blame me do he not live."

"Oh, he'll live," said the girl quickly. "Pearly is his name. We named him Pearly."

"Humph!" said Mary. "Well, you younguns head on to home."

"Don't forget he's ours," ventured Dovie.

Mary laughed a huge bellowing laugh. "Don't you fret none, girlie. I ain't hankering after another boy child to raise."

As they were passing down the steps a chunk of firewood flew above their heads, striking the back of Omer, who was bent over the rocks. "I didn't say rub, you no-count critter. I said scrub!" Mary roared.

Hallie stuck her fingers in her ears because Pearly M. Horton was wailing pitifully.

———

Mrs. Parker DeWitt, wife of the local minister, was not a person Hallie would ordinarily be glad to see. From her mother the girl had learned to be uncomfortable in the presence of the town's real ladies, owners of best and even second-best dresses. Still, there was relief for the girl when Mrs. DeWitt announced, "I've come to prepare the body."

Hallie had watched them move her mother back into the house, Mason lifting his wife while the boys hoisted the bed. It had been the same as in the morning. Only now the

Anna Myers

mountain breeze would not be missed by the still form, and the children whom she had wanted to hear at play sat silently on the porch, believing they would never play again.

Without a word to anyone their father had disappeared into the trees. For a time Hallie watched Starlin at work on the box. He wept openly, brushing at tears between the driving of each nail, and Hallie marveled at his freedom to do so. "I'm like Pa," she told herself, amazed at the realization. How could she be cut from the same cloth as the man who had been, always, a mystery to her?

Putting off the job of washing her mother, she first gave her attention to the burial clothing.

"Do up my other dress," her mother had told her the day before, but Hallie had refused to wonder why. She was heating the iron to give the dress a good pressing when Mrs. De-Witt came.

"I'll see to it all myself, child," said the woman, and Hallie noticed for the first time that her eyes were kind. Still, something made the girl shake her head.

"No, I ought not to leave her."

Mrs. DeWitt took from her bag some sweet-smelling oil, which she spread on the lifeless, just washed arms. "Poor soul," she whispered, half to herself, "worked to death she was."

Hallie, remembering Uncle Charlie's visit, felt her mother was being accused of something wrong. It had been five years earlier, just three weeks after the birth of Dovie.

Hallie was in the lot, about to drive the cow out to graze. Her mother, a bucket of milk in each hand, stopped suddenly in her struggle to get to the house. A man, strange to the girl, had appeared on horseback and was waving as he dismounted in front of the cabin.

"Mercy! It's your pa's brother Charlie." Her mother set down the buckets and nervously smoothed her hair. "Listen, we'll have to let on that the baby is two months old. It isn't fitting for a woman to get right up from childbirth and go to doing chores."

"No," said Hallie to Mrs. DeWitt, "Ma died of birthing trouble just like Mrs. Lafine herself did." Still, washing the callused hand of her mother, Hallie knew there was a difference. When Marie Lafine, daughter-in-law of the town's founder, had died, the schoolhouse was used for the funeral. Each of the older schoolgirls carried flowers to be placed around the casket. Hallie had seen Mrs. Lafine's ring-adorned hands resting across her breasts. They were nothing like the hands she washed now. Lifting one, she opened the palm and laid it, one last time, to her cheek.

Mrs. DeWitt touched Hallie's arm. "Poor child," she said. "You've lost the best friend you'll ever have in this world." She made a clucking sound with her tongue. "Be real hard for you to marry, too, leaving this bunch with no woman to do for them."

Hallie stood and bolted to the window. "I'm not hankerin' to marry up with no one." She wiped quickly at the tears forming in her eyes. There had been other longings, though, dreams, of an education. Hallie shrugged. No use thinking about such things.

The box was ready, sitting on the kitchen table. When Starlin began to spread Ma's wedding-ring-patterned quilt in the bottom, Hallie almost protested. She had spent many an hour studying the quilt and listening to her mother tell of its making, back in Arkansas, while she waited for the return of her trail driver. "It will be yours to keep when you marry," her mother had told her. But the boards were rough and the quilt was the best in the house. Hallie took an end to help with the spreading.

Mrs. DeWitt made a little snorting sound. "It just plain is not seemly, your pa deserting you at this time, leaving such things to children."

Hallie stiffened, but because of Starlin's quick, almost imperceptible, shake of the head, she said nothing. "Well, ma'am," he said softly, "Pa does like most other folks does. When he can't stand no more he bends. But Pa has to go off alone to do it. Reckon he figures it's better to leave us alone than to come apart before our eyes. Besides, I don't count myself a child, and Hallie here is full growed too."

Mrs. DeWitt smiled at him and reached out to give his arm a little squeeze. Hallie watched, as always without envy, but with great interest in Starlin's way with people. Had she responded even with those exact words, the woman's feathers would have been somehow ruffled.

Star, they had called him at school. And a star he was, on

the baseball diamond, with numbers on his slate, with everyone he met. To his sister he was the North Star, the only
direction left to her.

It was while they were moving the body into the box that
Hallie slipped out for the flowers. The slope behind the house
was thick with mountain daisies, but Hallie climbed just a
little farther to find the wild violets tucked between the rocks.
She gathered an apronful before heading back.

Sorry that Mrs. DeWitt was still in the room, Hallie kept
her eyes on her mother's face as she arranged the flowers
around the body. "They're violets, Ma." Her lips mouthed
the words. "They're violets. Can you smell them?"

"I don't know as I've ever seen flowers put right into the
box with the remains." Mrs. DeWitt's words interrupted her
silent communication, but still Hallie refused to look up.

"Ma was partial to violets," said Starlin in his slow, easy
way. "If it pleases Hallie to put them in, then I expect it
pleases Ma to have them."

"Well, sure," said the woman, certain now that a body
would be a fool not to see the truth of the boy's words.

When Mrs. DeWitt was at last gone, Hallie put sassafras
root on to boil. It had been her mother's way, tea when a
person was sick or downhearted. Hallie and Turner carried
the tea and crackers to the porch, where they would have
their supper. With water hauled from the creek, Starlin and
Brack were filling the big tub barrel that stood by the side
stoop. After the meal everyone would have a bath. The Hortons would not be found dirty at their mother's graveside.

Hallie woke the next morning to the sound of her father on the porch, sharpening his razor on the leather strop. Slipping from her narrow bed, more crowded than usual because sometime during the night Burch had climbed in beside Dovie, Hallie let herself out the side door and into her father's view.

"Best get the others to stirring," he said without greeting. "We'll needs be heading out soon."

In the kitchen, the girl stopped beside the box, surprised to see that the lid had been put in place during the night. The rocking chair, carried in from the yard, was beside the table. When she saw the lard can containing what looked to be a night's worth of her pa's pipe ashes, Hallie understood. As they slept, Mason had sat beside his wife and smoked his pipe. It was he who had closed the box after his private farewell.

"What can we eat?" Burch pulled at her dress.

"Are you hungry?" she asked. Suddenly, more than anything, she wanted one of her mother's biscuits, big, light, and golden brown. Well, they would have to make do with hers. And extra would be needed for the young ones to chew on during the long trip back. She was reaching for the biscuit board when she heard the noise of the wagon.

"Heidens!" one of the boys yelled from the yard.

So, Helga was coming! Hallie had longed for her friend but was surprised by the call so early in the day. Then an idea came to her. Maybe Helga would make biscuits. Motherless for some years, Helga's hands were quite efficient with the fry pan and the firebox.

She was in the yard when Hallie got there, a tall blond girl with braids wound around a plain face. "All young girls is pretty," Hallie had heard her mother say more than once in defense of Helga's looks.

The visitor set down a big, cloth-covered basket to put an arm around Hallie, who felt ashamed that she found even more comfort in the aroma from the basket than in the embrace.

Helga's young sister was unloading a big basket too. Their father, who ordinarily would have helped with the heavy containers, did not leave his place on the wagon seat. Since Kaiser Wilhelm had set out to build "a place in the sun" for Germany, Kurt Heiden, a German immigrant, was not always welcome in the homes of his neighbors.

Hallie thought him more than decent. There was a gentleness even in his hugeness, and she liked to hear the German phrases that appeared frequently in his speech. "*Mein Kind,*" he would say as he patted the head or shoulder of one of his daughters. To Hallie's ear the foreign words had a softness she longed to catch in her father's English.

"We're sure enough beholding for your kindness, sir," Starlin called up to Mr. Heiden.

"Oh, *ja, ja.*" His hand gestured the dismissal of any need for gratitude. "We know what it is. Nine years now my Marta has been gone." Then his face brightened. "Besides, only Helga it is to thank for the cooking. Some cook, my Helga."

Starlin turned to smile at the girl, whose answering smile was brief but resplendent. In that moment before Helga's eyes dropped for a deep study of the laces on her brown shoes, Hallie was amazed by two truths. Her mother had been right! Helga was pretty, but even more surprising was the fact that the newfound prettiness was a reflection of something passing between Helga and Starlin.

"Go on. Eat now," said the girl, stepping toward the wagon with Starlin quickly alongside to help her up, and before they had even rolled out of the yard, Hallie was giving the younger ones slices of smoked pork and biscuits kept warm by a hot brick. Helga had also packed fried chicken, two loaves of bread, raisin pudding, and a blackbery cobbler. Even Mason, reappearing after the Heidens' departure, had some appetite.

When they had eaten, the two little ones came to stand by Hallie while Mason and the boys loaded the box.

"Ma's in there," Dovie confided to Burch, who nodded his towhead in agreement, but still the little girl was compelled by the strangeness of it all to repeat the information. "Our Ma's right there in that box."

For a long time there was no conversation in the wagon, leaving only the noise of the wheels on the rocky road for accompaniment. Hallie wondered that she had never before recognized the terrible sadness of the sound. Dovie's words about the box returned to her thoughts, and putting out her

hand she touched the rough wood. Soon even that small opportunity for contact would be gone.

"Campfire," said Turner, pointing to smoke floating
above the trees.

"Childers having his breakfast, I reckon," said Brack.

Hallie turned her eyes from the smoke to the box again.
Childers had been a source of fretment to her mother. "Don't
you go looking for him none," she had cautioned the children. "Man running from the law, no telling what he might
do was he to be cornered." His campfires had worried her
too. "I hope he knows what he's doing," she would say when
the thin smoke was sighted. "A city fellow like that. Fire in
the hills can be a frightful thing."

"Most likely he's out there watching us right now."
Turner, whose legs were dangling from the back of the
wagon, shifted to be nearer Brack. The younger Hortons,
and even Hallie, had found some delight in the Childers tale.
Coming across an abandoned fire, they would poke at it and
marvel over an empty bean tin left behind. To them he was
more than a young man unwilling to fight a war in Europe.
He was the evil lurking in the trees, frightening, yet far
enough removed to be exciting.

But now Childers had lost his power to touch Hallie. He
was like a character in an uninteresting story. Let him live on
berries when the last bean tin was opened. Let him shiver
beside his miserable campfire through the mountain winter
to come. Hallie had cold enough of her own to cause a chill
in spite of the July sun.

Mason bent silently forward on the wagon seat, urging old Red and Doc on at a steady rate. When they were out of the hills, had passed by the Heiden farm at the base, and had driven through Lafine, they turned west on the smoother road toward their destination. It was the place Erwart Tanner, town storekeeper, postmaster, and gravedigger, had prepared a spot for Pearl Elizabeth Horton, wife of Mason, born October 3, 1880, died July 21, 1918.

The sun showed it was well into the afternoon when they pulled through the gates of the cemetery, named after the surrounding mountains and shared by Lafine and three neighboring communities.

Hallie, on her only previous visit to this site, had been fascinated by remembered stories of how early French explorers were first to leave their dead under these trees.

But on that earlier trip she had come out of curiosity, when her parents had felt compelled to help lay a neighbor, Columbus Crisswell, at last to rest.

"Always was peculiar," Ma had said. "Had to be, hankering to live way up there, not even a wagon road."

"True," Mason agreed, "but"—he nodded with pleasure—"Columbus didn't go plumb crazy till he got religion."

It was after the religion that Mrs. Crisswell had appeared one winter day at the Hortons' door. "My man is dead," she had said. They had brought her in and, warming by the fire, she had related the strange tale.

"Cut it off!" Columbus had said to his son, Lem.

"Aw now, Pa. That surely ain't right," Lem had argued.
"Now, Columbus always was powerful set in his ways,
and me and the boy done just about whatsomever he directed." The old lady turned to gaze into the fire. "Doubtless
I should have sided with the boy, but you've got to see the
way of it. Columbus declaring it was God's will and all. Why,
who was I to go against the Almighty and Columbus at one
turn? 'If Pa says cut it off, you better cut it off,' I told the
boy."

The Hortons had been shocked into silence. Hallie could
imagine the "boy" Lem, a simpleminded man not much
younger than her parents, raising the ax to remove his father's
leg.

"I want him to be laid alongside Christian folk," Mrs.
Crisswell had said, still staring into the fire. "That's a right
nice fire. Columbus sure could build good fires," she had
added cheerfully.

Mason had built a box and dragged it up and back
down the hill behind Doc. And so Hallie, who had begged
to go along, attended the burial of Columbus Crisswell, a
man who sure could build good fires. It was a phrase the
widow, proud of having thought of such a truthful tribute,
repeated often.

Remembering that earlier burial, Hallie felt shame for
having come out of curiosity. Preacher DeWitt was here at
her mother's grave just as he had been at crazy Columbus's,
and Hallie wondered why. Neither the Crisswells nor the

Hortons were real members of his congregation. It was duty then, she supposed, and duty now that brought the four ladies who came with him.

Hallie gave her head a shake and stared into their faces. Duty, she thought, was no better than curiosity. Those people cared nothing for her ma except, perhaps, for Mrs. Atkins, who would be concerned about the buttermilk.

"Your ma's buttermilk is the best there is," the woman said of the half gallon Hallie delivered each week, "and so clean."

Well, thought Hallie, almost smiling, it weren't so clean that once. Blackberries were ripe and Ma took the young ones off to pick, leaving Hallie in charge of the churning. Just a minute she was gone away from the churn and her spot on the porch to run into the house for a handful of yesterday's berries. Old Watch always followed the kids, but there he was when she came back out, his head in the churn, with only his ears sticking out on top.

Ma had looked at her closely when she refused buttermilk at supper, but Hallie hadn't confessed. Ma would have poured it out, and they needed the ten cents Mrs. Atkins would pay for her part. It was money Ma tucked away against things for her children, shoes once a year and, at Christmas, oranges. Once for Hallie there had been a china doll with coal black hair and painted blue eyes.

Likely Mrs. Atkins wouldn't want the milk now that Ma was gone. It was no matter; no one would want Christmas oranges either, without Ma.

Hallie jerked her mind away from what it could not endure and focused instead on Mrs. Atkins's shoes, a pair Hallie especially liked, black with shiny patent leather toes and trim. Even without closing her eyes the girl could picture the others in Mrs. Atkins's collection. Twice Hallie had seen them, having been invited to follow the woman into her bedroom while collecting the dime. They were on a shelf, at least six pair of them, and yet another pair on the lady's feet. Hallie had marveled openly, and everyone had listened when she told of them at supper.

"That's what I call sinful," Pa had grumbled, "being so prideful about your feet." But still, he had listened just like the young ones even to the account of the second viewing.

It was unnecessary to dwell too long on the shoes. A wagon rolled through the gate, and the preacher waited before opening his Bible. The Heidens came, bringing comfort to Hallie. Kurt Heiden was the most prosperous farmer around. He was able even to keep a hired hand, but he was careful. Probably not since his own wife's death had he left his fields on a workday. But they had come, Kurt to stand a few feet back with the team and little Kurin. Helga came to the graveside, tears in her eyes and carrying roses from her garden. It was right that there should be a real friend to mourn her mother, and Hallie was able to listen as Preacher DeWitt began to speak.

"Isaiah, chapter twenty-five, verse eight." Rev. DeWitt found it unnecessary to look down at his Bible to quote the scripture. "He will swallow up death in victory; and the Lord will wipe away tears from off all faces."

Hallie wondered if the preacher could quote all the Book or if this was a special verse learned by heart for funerals. Could he, she tried to remember, have used those same words for Columbus? They were grand words but gentle, too, and right for Ma, who had, in her lifetime, been supplied with many reasons to cry. They were right, too, for the tear-stained family. Hallie became aware that only she and her father were not weeping.

"Right hard-hearted, I reckon," the women would be saying in town, "a girl like that not even mourning for her ma."

"It's not so," Hallie wanted to call out. "I'm hurting sure enough. I'm grieving plenty." But she remained quiet and dry-eyed even when the box was lowered and she, like the others, had dropped handfuls of dirt to help cover it.

"Load on up," Mason ordered his children, as he lingered beside the newly covered mound, unable to join them. A hush was upon the waiting wagon. Hallie staring at her father's back as he knelt alone, was at first surprised and then angered to see his shoulders shaken by sobs. He's crying, she thought. Even Pa!

Star, moving to sit beside Hallie, put his arm around her. Finally, Mason pulled himself up. By the time he reached the wagon, his eyes were dry. Hallie stared at her father in wonder. When their gazes met, she thought she saw some sympathy, some understanding. But the moment was brief. "Got to get going," he shouted.

After a time she passed out cold biscuits and ham. Dusk

reached the hills just as the wagon did. To Hallie, the thought of coming upon the cabin with the moon shining and the night birds calling, coming home without Ma, seemed unbearable. When a whippoorwill cried out, she considered jumping to the ground and running until she dropped, running away from the hills. But there was Dovie, and Burch, and Turner, and of course, Pearly M. Horton. She would stay. At least she had Star, and so she could bear it, somehow.

2

THE DAYS THAT FOLLOWED were even hotter than usual, turning the mountain breeze into a dragon's breath. Glad for the cool water and for a reason to be away from the lonely cabin, the Horton young turned gratefully to the Mountain Fork. There the older boys, their workday shortened by the unrelenting sun, joined Hallie and the younger children each afternoon as soon as possible.

It was Hallie's habit to leave the stream then. There was no need for her watchful eye with Starlin present. Six years earlier, at only twelve, he had saved Hallie's life. Stepping unexpectedly into a deep hole, she had panicked and nearly drowned. Starlin, with her long hair wrapped around his hand, had been able to tow her to safety.

And so she would leave them splashing while she dressed quickly and uneasily in the thicket. Always she could feel the eyes of Gid Jones on her bare body. How could he know, she wondered, exactly where and when a girl was dressing or relieving herself among the trees? Yet she did not doubt he was out there, hidden in the greenness or behind a rock. "Gid's looking," was a phrase every hill girl associated with any form of nakedness.

Still, she would bow her neck, dress, and head for the very house that had produced the dreaded Gid.

"I've come to hold Pearly," she would say each day to Mary, who, when feeling friendly, would respond with a nod or a word of welcome. Often the woman would be too busy thundering at her husband, Shadrack, or throwing firewood at her sons to notice Hallie at all.

At first those trips to the Joneses' place had been almost too fear filled for Hallie to face. But gradually, like the menfolk who lived there, Hallie began to pay little attention to Mary's shouts and was able even to laugh about it all with Helga and Starlin.

"They don't give much heed till she commences to throw things," Hallie told them. "But I'll say this for her, she's right respectful of Shadrack. Him being the head of the house, she won't chuck firewood at him, just kindling and fry pans."

Often Hallie thought of her mother's words, "Now, Mary is hard and rough, but her young ones is always fat." It was true. A rougher woman the girl could not imagine, but it was no matter. Pearly M. Horton was growing fat, would be fatter even, Hallie believed, than young Woodrow Jones.

"His pa named that one after the president, I reckon," Mary said one day of the baby as if he were a stranger. "That's plumb peculiar, Shadrack being a Republican." She paused for the spit that punctuated almost every sentence. "Well, I'll tell you, that young one coming is right strange all around. Wouldn't you have figured me and his pa was done with such nonsense as baby making?"

Hallie looked quickly away from the woman to count Pearly's toes. Maybe, she thought, one of the boys will come in and set her off to swearing again. Anything would be better than to be taken so embarrassingly into Mary's confidence.

The girl searched for something to say. "Do you suppose Woodrow will have black hair like Gid and Olie or red like Erbie and Omer?" It was true she wanted to change Mary's train of thought, but the question was born, too, from sincere interest in Woodrow's future hair. Would he, she wondered, become a "black bastard" or a "red bastard"? The labels were ones Mary was fond of shouting at her sons.

A great laugh preceded Mary's joke. "Well," she cackled, "maybe he'll just stay bald and be like his pa."

When the opportunity arose, Hallie took little Pearly and slipped out to a bench near the smokehouse. It was quiet there, and she could coo privately with the baby. She rocked him to and fro in her arms and sang as she had done so often during the first days of his life, but the songs had changed. Too painful now were those other ones, melodies learned from her mother. Instead she turned to words taught her by the girls at school.

> *"I will tell you a story of a pretty white rose.*
> *It is true, but oh, how sad.*
> *Of a cruel, cruel woman whose heart was made of stone,*
> *but oh, how she flirted with that lad.*

He was found one morning in a cold, cold stream
where he threw himself there to drown;
With that rose between his teeth
as if he seemed to say,
I want to wear this rose in my crown."

While she sang, Hallie studied the tiny face, bending occasionally to kiss the fat cheeks or forehead.

"Just like a songbird." Gid was leaning on a nearby tree, and Hallie froze with her head down at the sound of his voice. "Why don't you look up at me, girlie? Then you might not be having to spend so much time kissing on a baby."

Her head did go up then, and her voice was unquivering. "If you was to ever so much as touch me, Gid Jones, my brother would kill you."

Suddenly Mary was there, stepping from around the smokehouse corner with a rifle in her hand. "No," she roared, "your brother would have no call to be hurting Gid. I'd have done shot the black bastard my ownself!" A bullet flew over the boy's head and he ran.

Hallie was barely able to breathe, but Mary, perfectly relaxed, eased herself down to sit beside the girl and leaned the gun between them. "That one bears watching." She shook her head wonderingly. "I can't fathom why. Maybe I've been too easy on him."

And so summer stacked its last days one on top of the other. For Hallie each day began with the same ritual. Waking pleasantly to the song of the mockingbird from the pear tree, she would ignore the thought pushing at her mind. Stretching her toes slowly to the end of her short bed, she would yawn luxuriously and roll over. Only then did she face the truth hammering at her consciousness. "Ma is dead. Our ma is in that box." It came to her each morning, cruelly new and devastating.

She would lie, staring at the beams above her and pondering how that huge truth had changed them all—the cabin and its inhabitants. Meals were different. Hallie lacked her mother's power to take the simple yield of field and wilderness and turn it into food that satisfied their hunger.

"Ain't it funny," said Turner, who had been released from field work to help Hallie with canning, "seems like the apples just don't smell as good this year."

Dovie and Burch spoke of their mother with more ease than did the others. "How big do you reckon Ma's wings are?" Dovie asked often.

If Burch caught a fair-sized fish, he would look searchingly toward the sky. "Sure hope Ma can see this one."

Their grief was more open too. "I want my ma," from one of the little ones plunged Hallie into the deepest agony. Starlin, gathering a small body to him, would rock it while crying silently, but Hallie's sorrow lay like a lump of rain-soaked feathers in a blue ticking pillow, retrieved too late from its airing. When the wad of pain became unbearable, the girl would slip with it out the kitchen door and climb above the rocky, hillside farm to a spot where the creek narrowed before dropping into the hollow. Drawn by the call of water over boulders, she would settle on the grassy bank, giving up the sounds of her despair and mixing them with the rush of the Mountain Fork.

Later, she would lie on her back, exhausted, and study the summer sky. "Ma," she would whisper weakly. "Ma, you had no call to go off and leave us."

It was there once that she saw the figure among the trees, not far from where she lay. He was tall, young and broad of shoulder. Having cried out all her tears, she was pushing herself up to a sitting position when the blue of his shirt caught her eye.

Don't move sudden like, she told herself. Don't give him a start. There was in her mind no doubt. It was Childers. The fugitive from the draft had been watching her, had heard her sorrow. A strange idea came to the girl, the impulse to hold out her hand. He knows grief too, she thought. Might be she would just call his name, real gentle. Might be he would come sit beside her, but then he was gone, disappeared behind the trees.

Hallie was able to join the others in what she supposed was an attempt to fill the empty space by using phrases that were decidedly Ma's. "Sorry as white dog manure," one of the boys would say when describing an unfit person or object.

"All young girls is pretty," Hallie told Dovie as she brushed the child's hair.

"Keep your head up even if you do die hard," Starlin would say to urge on a younger brother. But the emptiness would not be filled, and it drove Mason further and further from the family who needed him. Only once was the indifference in which he wrapped himself pulled away.

"Pa! Pa!" Brack came running into the cabin about dusk. "Harp Otis is coming up the trail. He's got a gun, and he's got Turner!"

Mason dropped his pipe. "Burch, Dovie, go to the back room. Get under a bed and stay there, no matter what. Brack, get my gun and stay to the side of the window. Don't show yourself or the gun unless forced. Starlin, take your gun and circle around so as to be behind Harp. Hallie, you come with me. Might be the sight of a young girl will calm him."

Hallie doubted it. If Harp Otis was riled, it seemed unlikely he would be soothed by looking at a puny girl. A huge, silent man, he had appeared in Lafine a few years earlier and bought a small farm on the outskirts of town, down the road from the Heidens. Harp Otis, he was called, but no one knew if Otis was his last or first name or if he used the name Harp because he carried a harmonica. Those who happened to have heard him play on the trail or in his yard at night said the music was beautiful.

His left leg was lame, from a mine cave-in, some said. Others claimed he had been injured in a shoot-out where two men had been killed over in Latimer County. But not a soul considered asking Harp what had really happened. He had piercing dark eyes, and when Harp came to shop at the Lafine store, one of his glances could drive any child and most men from it.

Hallie walked behind her father as they went out to meet

Harp, who stood with one heavy hand on Turner's shoulder. In the other hand was a gun. "The boy took my horse." Harp released Turner long enough to give him a resounding thump in the back with a massive thumb.

"What's this?" Mason thundered. He reached for Turner, but Harp's hand was back on the shoulder and drawing the boy possessively closer.

Hallie looked for a terrifying second at the giant and then began to search the trees for a glimpse of Starlin.

"I didn't meant to swipe him or nothing, Pa." There was a whiteness visible on Turner's face in spite of his tan. "I just come acrost him on the trail, and I aimed to ride him just a space. That was all. But the fool thing . . ."

Harp's gun was in the boy's ribs. "Feather ain't no fool thing!"

"Easy, now wait, Harp. I'd be obliged if you'd see your way clear to put down your gun. Turner here is just . . ."

"Nine," supplied Hallie, knowing her father was searching for an age.

"Yes, just nine. I don't reckon the boy meant no harm." Mason looked meaningfully at Turner.

"Lord, let him say something sensible," Hallie prayed silently.

"No, sir! I did not. I sure enough did not mean no harm. This is a powerful smart horse and fast, too. I was just hankering to set up on him for a time and feel proud. That was all, but he paid my direction no heed. Just laid back his ears and ran fast to your door."

"A right smart horse." Mason laughed a nervous laugh, and Harp joined with a deep chuckle.

"No, sir," said Mason, reaching now to put his arm around Turner. "My boys ain't likely to turn to thieving horses, but was they to sink that low, I reckon they wouldn't start with yourn."

"No, sir," said Turner. Hallie was fascinated by the smile that lit Harp's face.

"Come on in, Harp," said Mason. "We got some berry cobbler that is sure enough good."

It was an event the children would recount many times. Harp Otis eating berry cobbler in their own cabin and then playing "Red-Wing" on his harmonica.

———

ON A SUNDAY AFTERNOON another incident occurred. They had not intended to go to the rally, had not even known the government man was in town to encourage the sale of liberty bonds and to urge the saving of food. Chores were finished. Hallie sat with the others in the yard, alternately studying the ground and the limbs of the shade tree.

Once Sunday with its slacking of chores had been Hallie's favorite day. On summer Sundays, Ma had often settled under a tree with beans to snap or mending to do. Gradually, the children would collect themselves on the ground around her, drawing pictures in the dirt, waiting for Ma's stories to begin.

But now, Hallie thought, Sundays ain't nothing to shout about. She did sit under a shade tree, but her fingers, slow and awkward with the needle, gave up and lay idle in her lap. Nor did her mind turn to storytelling. What did she know to tell?

The children about her shared her unhappy mood. "That ain't your steely," Burch complained from where he and Turner had begun a game of marbles.

"Is so," Turner shouted.

"Ain't neither!" Burch jumped up and stomped a bare foot into the marble ring.

Hallie shook her head in exasperation. "Might be I'll just put you both to chopping weeds, Sunday or no."

It was Starlin who improved everyone's humor. "Almost train time," he called, coming into the yard from the barn. "Just as well go over and watch."

Twice a day the Fort Smith and Western came through Lafine, providing the town with some measure of excitement. Children and adults would go down to the depot to watch the train pull in and out, and to stare into the windows at the mysterious travelers. On still evenings with the right wind, the sound of the whistle carried over the hills to the Horton cabin.

But when they arrived in town there was a stir too big to be caused by a train. A crowd had gathered at the school where crude benches were set up. Two large signs stood on either side of the steps. One said, "Blood or Bread. Others are giving their blood. Wheat is needed for the Allies." The other had a picture of serious young soldiers with guns and read, "You buy a Liberty Bond. We will do the rest."

On the steps were two men, and one of them was playing a harmonica. Hallie, with Dovie and Burch in tow, stopped near the back of the crowd, just over to the edge so that the little ones could see. Turner and Brack squirmed their way through to be close to the front, and Starlin moved to the middle to share a bench with Helga, her father, and her sister.

The notes of "America the Beautiful" reached out to Hallie, who thrilled to the music and to the words she recited in her mind. They were lucky, she thought, to have happened upon such an interesting event.

Even when Mrs. Tanner, as head of the ladies' committee, was called upon to speak, Hallie listened with pleasure.

The woman pushed nervously at her hat. "Like Mr. Steele says, we got to buy bonds and savings stamps, and remember, don't come in to the store and ask for flour on Wheatless Thursdays." She was relaxing now, enjoying the sound of her voice. "If you was to ask for flour on a Thursday, why, we would just have to refuse, and what is more, others would hear and think you don't care about your country."

The government man, obviously ready to take charge again of the program, eased himself up to stand beside Mrs. Tanner. She, however, ignored him and talked on. "And too there's comfort pillows, which is what us ladies make for sol-

diers. Just save back all your white scraps from sewing. A
soldier's head can rest more easy on our pillows."

"Hey," yelled a voice from the crowd. "We can do more
than save scraps and cut back on wheat." Suddenly Elton
Holmes had pushed his way to the front and up the steps. He
was a no-account man younger than Hallie's father but a deal
older than Star. Sometimes he worked in the mines, sometimes at the sawmill, but mostly he fought and drank. Before
he spoke, he wiped the tobacco from his mouth onto his shirtsleeve. "Men," he shouted. "We got to get that slacker." He
inclined his head in the direction of the hills. "It ain't right,
letting him hide up there."

"That's right." Hallie couldn't see who was talking, but
she knew it was one of Elton's cohorts. "And Germans. Hell,
there's a German right here. Had the nerve to show his rotten
face at a meeting for decent Americans."

Delight in the Sunday outing was gone. Hallie stared
ahead, horrified, as Elton made a fist and thrust it into the
air. "Down with Germans and slackers," he yelled.

The government man said something, but the uproar in
the crowd kept Hallie from hearing. Then she realized that
Star was moving quickly up the steps. "Oh, Lord," she whispered. "They'll fight sure enough." Clearly, the other Horton
boys agreed with her prediction. Brack and young Turner
were standing, ready to take on the first comer.

But Star ignored Elton. Holding up his arms, he shouted,
"Please." The crowd quieted somewhat.

"Let him talk," yelled a man who was on Star's ball team.

His voice was steady and warm. "Folks, let me tell you how it is with Kurt Heiden. Sure, he was born in Germany, but I've been at his table. Heard him pray for peace and for the safe return of our soldiers."

"Starlin Horton tells things straight," called another voice from the crowd. Hallie could feel the electricity of anger soften.

"How about another song?" said the government man, and the harmonica began again. Hallie could find no joy in the music. Quickly and with heads down, the three Heidens were moving out of the crowd and toward their wagon.

3

STARLIN'S STONY EXPRESSION kept the other children quiet on the ride home. Never saw him act like Pa before, Hallie thought, as she watched him hunch silently forward on the wagon seat, but she shook her head to quiet Burch's and Dovie's questions.

By breakfast the next morning Star was himself again, and Elton's threats provided the morning talk. "You going to have to whip him?" Turner asked his brother.

The older boy smiled as he poured syrup over his biscuits. "Fellows like that mostly blow. Don't usually come to a real fight."

"Some fools looking to use the war as excuse to do what decent folks wouldn't tolerate during regular times," Mason commented.

"Reckon the Heidens are fixing to get hurt?" It was Turner's question, and Hallie, waiting to hear the answer, froze at the stove, where she had gone for more mush.

"Likely the Heidens will be pretty much staying clear of town from now. Expect they'll send the hand for what they got to have."

Hallie turned her head to look out the kitchen window toward the pines. Maybe staying away from town was the answer. Maybe the war and the crazy things it made people do would stay out of their hills.

"But ball games. The Heidens can still go to ball games, can't they?" Burch pulled at his brother's arms.

"Why, sure." Star patted the boy's head. "There ain't going to be no trouble at the ball field, and I suspect it's about time I got back to playing."

Star had missed the first two ball games following his mother's death. "Couldn't settle my mind on it," he told the teammates who came to urge him.

Dovie jumped down from the table and scurried to get his red shirt with the stitched-on white letters reading LAFINE, OKLAHOMA.

"Next Sunday for sure," Star told them when the little girl handed him the shirt. "There's a game next Sunday, and we'll all go, right, Pa?"

Baseball was one of the few things outside the hillside farm to which Mason paid any heed. "Sure as the dickens," he told the young ones. "Come next Sunday we'll all load up and see us a ball game."

There was no further mention of Elton Holmes. All week the children talked of the coming ball game, but the uneasy feeling inside Hallie would not go away.

Finally, when Sunday did come, she began to feel a little better. Part-time sawmill wages had allowed Starlin to purchase a horse, which he would ride on ahead. Watching him mount the shiny black animal to ride away, waving his baseball cap, made Hallie feel lighter than she had ever expected to feel again.

It was the first happiness the family had experienced since Ma's death. "Don't it set strange to be so glad?" Turner asked Hallie as they rode along. "Is it bad, do you reckon?"

"Why, no." The girl smiled at him. "Ma never wanted to go to games anyway," she added as if that were the issue.

Pa pulled into a spot with a good view. Hardly had they stopped when another wagon, belonging to their neighbors, pulled up close beside theirs. Ruby Willbanks drove the team with her mother and older sister, Vida Mae, beside her. Mrs. Willbanks stood and scooted Vida Mae to the middle of the seat in order to be nearer Mason.

"I've been hankering to express my sympathy upon your sorrow," she said as demurely as possible, while leaning toward the man.

"Thank you, ma'am." Mason searched the empty ball field as if a gripping game were in progress.

"It's a powerful heartbreak when a dear one is snatched away so sudden like. That's how it were with Cal, don't you know." Smothering a laugh, Hallie turned her head away. Yes, they knew how it was when Cal Willbanks was "snatched away." Hallie had heard it straight from Ruby, who was inclined to tell family secrets.

"Head for the smokehouse, kids," Buna Willbanks had yelled with joy when the old man drew his last breath. No one blamed her. Working the fields themselves for years had not given the woman or her daughters the right to eat meat or do anything else without the permission of Calvin.

But Hallie found the woman's new interest in Mason to be a great amusement. My pa don't rightly need no ties, she considered telling the woman.

Because Vida Mae was well past the age most hill girls married, Mrs. Willbanks had given a party last Christmas inviting every eligible young man and presenting each with a gaily wrapped necktie. They came, according to Ruby, from the attic of Mr. Lafine, for whom Buna Willbanks worked. Even Star, years younger than Vida Mae, had been given one, and it reeked with the smell of cleaning fluid.

It seemed now that Mrs. Willbanks had consigned Vida Mae to the ranks of hopeless spinsters and was turning her attention to finding a replacement for Calvin.

"Were I to be a help in any way"—the woman folded her hands under her chin—"you'd need but to summon me, don't you know."

"Thank you, ma'am," said Mason, climbing out of the wagon without looking at her. "See yonder." He turned to the children. "Want to go see the players limber up over yonder?"

It was just then that the Heiden wagon rolled into the field. "Damn Kraut," came a shout from a group of men who stood a few feet away.

Hallie held her breath. Maybe Star was wrong about peace at the ball game. She shaded her eyes to see the wagon. The Heidens must have had a real hankering to see Star play ball. They sat straight on their seats and did not turn their heads to either side.

Star stopped his warm-up long enough to walk over to where Kurt Heiden had pulled his big horses to stop just inside the gate. Hallie kept her eyes on her brother, and her muscles began to relax. Here at the ball field he was powerful important. Folks would not want to argue with Star for fear he might refuse to play. Hallie watched him speak briefly with the Heidens, then go back to the field ready to start the game. Star would take care of everything again. Thank heavens for Star.

No more echoes of rage came from the crowd, and Helga came undisturbed to share Hallie's wagon seat. Hallie watched her friend's approach and wondered what words of comfort to use in the face of the community hatred.

But Helga had other things to talk about. "See that red handkerchief in Star's pocket?" Her eyes were aglow. "I made it, and he promised to have it at every game."

"Your pa don't mind then?"

"He's real pleased." Helga reached for her friend's hand. "You are too, Hallie, aren't you?"

"Sure enough. Could be we'll just end up sisters." Ashamed of how she really felt, Hallie looked quickly away from the other girl. Now Helga and Star were turning to each other. Once Hallie had believed there was a real man in the moon. Suddenly, she knew it was after all a girl who sat removed from everyone, a girl so unspeakably lonely.

Not until they were on the way home did Hallie realize

she had forgotten to tell Helga about Mrs. Willbanks. Oh well, like as not it would have lost some of the humor in the repeat. Besides, since the last game, Helga had developed a powerful new interest in what happened on the baseball field.

The wagon was full of baseball talk all the way home. "Did you see . . ." Brack or Turner would begin and elaborately recount some detail of the game as though the others had not been there.

Little Burch tried several times unsuccessfully to break into the conversation. Finally a lull came, and he shouted quickly, "Dovie, did you know I'm fixing to be a pitcher, too? Me and Starlin is going to be partner pitchers."

It was because Dovie, who was rarely to be outdone, made no response that Hallie looked closely at the little girl and noticed for the first time the red cheeks and glassy eyes. Scooting across to the child, she laid her face against the child's to confirm the fever.

"My chest hurts," Dovie said, and she moved to settle in her sister's lap.

Hallie remembered then noticing a runny nose at breakfast. "Pa," she called to Mason. "I reckon Dovie's down with a cold and already feverish."

Mason looked back at them over his shoulder. "Summer cold," he said, as if the words had always been his and not a saying of his dead wife's. "Summer cold is hard to come by and harder still to shake."

Before they were home, Hallie knew that it was even

worse than a summer cold. Dovie's raspy cough left no room for doubt, and Hallie felt unreasonably put out with the child. What call did Dovie have getting the croup now that Ma was gone? It was a condition not to be reckoned with lightly.

Finally Starlin, who came home at dusk, was sent to fetch Mary Jones. Hallie would have felt better loading Dovie up for a trip to see the doctor in Stigler. It seemed unlikely that the black or red bastards had ever been brave enough to plague Mary Jones with the croup. Hallie also disliked thinking of Pearly left with only the Jones boys or Shadrack to tend him.

However, Mary, when she arrived, brought not only knowledge for treating croup but also a large wicker basket containing a sleeping baby at each end.

"Oh, you have them with you." Hallie cleared a place on the kitchen table.

"Lands, yes, girl. I'd sooner leave babies with the hounds than with that wild Jones bunch!" Mary issued a cabin-shaking laugh, but the babies, well used to the noise, slumbered on. "Now," she continued in a businesslike voice, "we got to get a hold on that devil croup. You boil water for steam and heat this here skunk oil for rubbing whilst I mix the elixir. And I'm in need of something for spitting." Looking down she added, "I'd not spit on nary a floor, even iffen it wants scrubbing like yourn does."

The floor *was* dirty. Hallie felt ashamed and angry. Her body ached with tiredness. It was too much—the cabin, the meals, the croup, and Mary Jones criticizing Ma's floor. To-morrow Hallie would make someone clean it even if she had to throw firewood at them!

Pa had moved a cot into the kitchen for Dovie, whose chest rattled as Mary and Hallie rubbed on the warm skunk oil. A terrible fear came to Hallie. "Will she die?" The girl was unable to raise her questioning eyes to the woman's face.

"No, child." Mary's voice was strangely gentle. "You won't have that to bear. Not this time." She laid a cloth, warmed from the stove, on Dovie's chest, smoothing it with a large hand. "A little one's death do be a terrible thing. I know."

It was late. The cabin was quiet and dark except for the island of light from the lamp at one end of the kitchen. The unreality of it all gave Hallie unusual courage. She was about to ask Mary for more information, but after a spit into the can provided for that purpose, Mary went on without urging.

"I had me a little girl oncet." She stroked Dovie's fore-head with a wet cloth. "Pretty little thing. So pretty. Not even as old as this one she weren't when we lost her."

Hallie was amazed! No one had ever spoken of a Jones girl. "I didn't know you and Shadrack had a girl. Was she the oldest?"

"She weren't Shadrack's. Didn't I tell you she were pretty?" Mary started to laugh her usual bellow but stopped. "No, girl, I don't hardly tell this story because Shadrack ain't never heard it." She spat into the can. "It might trouble him some that there weren't no end to that first marriage, making his boys bastards and all."

Mary sat back in her chair, and her voice took on a softness Hallie would not have believed possible. "Over in Arkansas it were. Not far from Fort Smith. My man worked at the mines bringing up coal. William were his name, and our baby girl we called Lucy. They was both so pretty and fine." Mary reached across to touch the girl's arm. "I was too, child, though likely you won't believe it. Pretty and soft like I was. William, he wouldn't know me, was we to meet again. All the softness went out of me way back then." As if to punctuate the last sentence, the woman spat hard into the can.

"Summer it were, and we was in town going into the store. Lucy spied some shiny red shoes in the window. Held out her little foot and asked for them, but we hushed her and said maybe next time. We bought some flour and coffee and that lye. There weren't no need to buy much else. We had the finest garden you ever did see. There was money left, enough for the shoes, but we just got her a peppermint, and she didn't say nothing more. Sweet thing. She weren't spoiled at all, even with everyone making over her all the time on account of her being so pretty.

"I worked in the kitchen when we got home, putting up tomatoes. William was plumb partial to tomatoes. Why he started making up the soap has always plagued me. There weren't nothing said between us concerning starting right then. But he done it. Stirred up the lye and left it in the kettle with that big dipper. Left it all, and went off to the barn without a thought about that baby."

Hallie could find nothing to say, and Mary seemed not to expect a comment. "We bought the shoes. William went to town and got the store man to open up and sell him them red shoes. I put 'em on her feet myself. So shiny. After she was in the ground, I just walked off. Waited till no one were watching and just started walking."

She paused now and looked at Hallie. "It weren't blaming William that made me go. Just weren't nothing left to stay for, nothing left inside me. Got a ride after a time and went to a boarding house in Fort Smith. The woman there was right kind, let me work for my keep. After a time Shadrack come along, and I figured why not team up with him." Mary stood up. "One thing though. I always wondered about the garden, as to iffen William tended to it, or just let it go." She spit into the can. "Lands, child, I sure was took by a talking spell. Think I'll try a shot of that elixir my ownself."

Hallie trembled as she passed the jar. She was overwhelmed. Mary, even Mary Jones, had churnings inside her, feelings she had laid out there in the lamplight. The ache in the girl was magnified. It was an ache for Mary and her lost Lucy, for little Dovie who muttered "Ma" in her sleep, and most of all for herself, mortally wounded, but unable to say so. Tentatively she laid her hand on the woman's shoulder, and Mary patted it as she swigged down the yellow elixir.

4

DOVIE MENDED QUICKLY and by the next evening only a cough and a peaked look remained of her illness.

"There's cold biscuits, tater pie, and buttermilk. Tonight it's every dog for his own self," Hallie declared at suppertime. Later she settled with Dovie on the pallet spread near the door to catch the breeze.

Making her expression as wan as possible, the little girl pulled on her sister's arm. "Read to me, please." She pushed the fair hair back from her forehead. "I'm feeling poorly again." Her voice was weak.

"Dovie Horton, you're a puredee put-on!" Hallie stretched to the rough shelf that held the Bible and Hallie's book. Often Hallie pretended reluctance to read aloud to the younger children when, in truth, she delighted in every word of the Grimm fairy tales. Even holding the book caused a pleasant sensation. When only the little ones were in the room with her, she would begin by reading aloud the inscription. "To Hallie upon winning the spelling bee. Dream big and your dreams will carry you over all mountains. Your teacher, Elizabeth Clark."

Sweet, pretty Miss Clark. Hallie wondered often about her. Was she still in Tulsa where she had gone when she left

Lafine? "It's a bigger place," Miss Clark had said. "I won't be dismissed in Tulsa because I believe women should vote."

Hallie had hoped the women would make the school board change their minds about firing such a wonderful teacher, but the protest had been mostly whispered. "Ought to be a woman on that school board," Mrs. Atkins had told Hallie when she'd delivered buttermilk. "Womenfolk around here got to learn to stand up for what's right. I'm not the only one thinks so either. You mark my words."

Hallie had marked them and hoped, but Miss Clark left. Her leaving broke Hallie's heart and resulted in many bruised boys, because in her place had come the dreaded Theodore Preston, who, until his recent departure, had been the most hated man in Lafine.

"Don't get me, Mr. Preston," was the mumbled theme of many a childhood nightmare. Great red marks from shoulder to knee were an indication that a boy had been "got" by Mr. Preston for nodding off to sleep during lessons or for laughing. Always suspicious of being laughed at, Mr. Preston would not tolerate even an unexplained smile.

"I just might have to commence on a new policy. No need to exempt girls from discipline," he threatened, but only Ruby Willbanks had actually been struck and then only on the hands. It was the general opinion that Ruby had been selected because she was fatherless.

Mr. Preston was a short, stocky man, with strong arms. The real sources of his power, however, were his eyes and voice—cold, hard, and as terror inspiring as the great leather strap never out of sight while school was kept.

"We'll get him," was a muttered threat on the lips of almost every schoolboy. "Someday we'll get Mr. Theodore Preston right good," they said, but never very loudly.

Finally, on the last literary evening of the school term, things changed. Clarice Tanner was reciting "Psalm of Life" when Ruby punched Hallie.

"Brack just snuck into the cloakroom," Ruby whispered, "and I seen Jake and Folbert going in a while back."

Hallie's eyes searched quickly and found Mr. Preston in the second row, nodding encouragement to his special favorite, Clarice. Special enough, it was rumored, as to cause his hand to rest on her knee when she sat beside his desk for help with numbers.

"Mr. Preston don't know they're in there," Hallie whispered back, but she lost all interest in Mr. Longfellow's poetry and in the following pieces. What were the boys up to? Anything, anything at all, would warrant a beating from Mr. Preston. And if Brack got into trouble, Ma and Pa might not allow the children to sally forth to future social functions. Already Ma, who felt uncomfortable with what she thought of as city folk, would attend only the Christmas gathering. Hallie knew Ma went at Christmas because the little ones begged to see the tree. She also knew Ma felt uneasy about the amount of mixing the older children were doing.

Even the courting line formed outside after the program

did not give Hallie its usual pleasure. Normally, she would, like the other girls, look out the window and giggle over which boys were successful with their "see you home?" and which boys were "stung," a word used to indicate refusal.

Not until the wagon had crossed the first mountain did Hallie feel removed enough from the scene to whisper the question to Brack. "Cut up that damn strap!" Brack answered, trying to sound brave. The knife he took from his pocket gleamed in the moonlight. "Cut it up in tiny pieces and put them in his hat!"

Brack was nervous but not terrified. "This just might be the end of Mr. Theodore Preston," he confided to Hallie. "It just might be!" He had adamantly refused to let Hallie tell Star. "Me and Jake has a plan." His face was grim but determined.

"I know who has done this," roared Mr. Preston first thing Monday morning. His coat was off, and the rolled sleeves of his shirt revealed the hairiest of all arms. "I have my ways, and I know who has done this thing." A massive, thatch-covered arm pushed a fist into the air. "You shall be chastised, chastised here and now!"

"With what, Mr. Preston, sir?" It was Brack's voice, but Hallie was too frightened to turn and look at him.

"Yeah, with what?" Jake was rising from his place in front of Hallie, who now found the courage to look around the room to see four of the other big boys stand too.

Mr. Preston's face was red, and Hallie half expected to see smoke come from his nose. "I shall speak to the school board about this. School is dismissed for the day," he said before stomping out the back door. Mr. Preston, the children learned later, returned to McCurtain, leaving only Clarice Tanner to mourn his going. And so, summer vacation had begun three weeks early.

"Having no teacher at all is better than having Theodore Preston," townfolk had said to console each other when no new teacher had been found by August.

"It's the war," Pa said. "Young men gone off to fight, leaving lots of jobs open for lady teachers and older men. Might take a spell to find a teacher needing a job enough to come to Lafine."

While Hallie continued to read from Grimm, she was aware of Star on the porch, softly singing "Old Dan Tucker," while he washed. Going courting again! Hallie disliked the resentment that came to her like bile from a sick stomach. Ashamed, she longed to find joy in this new relationship between her brother and her best friend. "Yes, ain't it grand?" she had answered Ruby's question when they met at the store, but it was loneliness she felt! Star was going to Helga's house, and neither of them would wish that Hallie were with them.

After the young ones were asleep, she slipped out to a big rock near the hitching post. To the south, about halfway up the mountain, was the glow of a small campfire. "Go pester Childers," Hallie said to old Watch, who, still upset by Starlin's refusal of his company, whimpered his complaint to the girl as she settled herself on the rock to stare at the full moon.

"Dad-blamed moon!" she muttered, reaching back to the

old resentment she had felt years earlier upon learning there was no man. Pa had made real for her the unfortunate creature sentenced to lunar isolation for burning trash on Sunday.

He had added quickly, "Of course the Lord does understand when a man has a passel of hungry mouths to feed, but that fellow"—he shifted the load of wood to one arm in order to point at the moon—"he were a bachelor." Regarding it as a special confidence between her and Pa, Hallie had hated giving up the story.

Everything about those days had been easier, more carefree. "Happy Hollow" they called the space between the two mountains occupied by the Hortons, Joneses, Willbanks, and partway up the next hill, the Crisswells. Happy it had been for Hallie until death disfigured everything and romance had added its changes.

"Well," she sighed aloud and shifted on the rock, "maybe I'll just have to try my hand at spooning." There was always young Erwart Tanner, son of the storekeeper and younger brother of Clarice. Erwart was seventeen, a year older than Hallie, but two terms behind her at school. In spite of the fact that the boy had already inherited his mother's chin, an item missing on the faces of his sister and their father, and in spite of the fact that he would inherit his father's business, Hallie had never taken to Erwart. But it was no secret that he was sweet on her.

Two years earlier he had asked to see her home from a doings at the schoolhouse. "Quite a walk for a prairie dog," Star had teased as the boy and girl waved his wagon on.

"I reckon I can cross hills as good as you mountain boomers," Erwart had retorted, but his steps had become very slow and his breathing hard before the trail ended at the cabin door.

"I'll wager that prairie dog won't make it back to town till next week," Star had laughed. Unwilling to miss any opportunity for fun, the younger boys had followed Erwart for a time, sneaking through the trees and issuing cougar imitations. Still, Hallie knew he had made it home because Pa had sent her to town for nails the next day.

"Can I help you?" the boy had asked, smiling all over himself. Hallie was glad Star could not see Erwart's limp.

"I'll see to the girl." Mrs. Tanner pushed her son aside. "You get to your studies. Bright boy like you has got no time to waste." She gave Hallie a fake smile.

There had been no other offers to escort Hallie home in spite of the fact that young Erwart now drove his father's rig to socials. But there were smiles aplenty, and frequently peppermints had appeared mysteriously on Hallie's desk. With just a little encouragement, Hallie believed, the boy would ignore his mother's disapproval and, if necessary, carry Hallie across the mountain!

But Hallie hadn't cared enough to fight Mrs. Tanner's unwillingness to accept her. "Strings!" the girl had heard Erwart's mother say disparagingly with a nod in their direction as she and Ruby had passed a group of women at a schoolhouse gathering.

Well, Hallie thought, maybe I am stringy. Poor people

have poor ways, Ma always says. But at the time, Hallie had a plan to show them all. Encouraged by Miss Clark, she had a secret dream of becoming a teacher after attending normal school at Tahlequah. Even Mr. Preston had been impressed with her scores on the eighth grade county exam.

"I might have friends who could help a girl like you," he had told her.

Dropping her eyes quickly to her slate, Hallie had only nodded, certain in the knowledge that her leg would rot off if ever touched by Mr. Preston.

Anyway, Mr. Preston was gone now, and the new teacher, if one ever came, would not know Hallie at all. Dreams, she supposed, were like stories about the moon, things to leave behind with childhood.

She would, undoubtedly, remain in the cabin with her silent father until the young ones were grown. Then, like Mary Jones, perhaps she would just start walking.

5

IT WAS ALMOST SEPTEMBER, and still the air among the trees lay thick and warm like an unwanted blanket. As an escape Hallie sought the cool darkness of the cellar, where she lingered over the churning and tried to ignore the sparsity of canned goods put away against winter. Ma, the girl knew, would have shaken her head and talked about Hunger like an intruder waiting to enter the cabin.

Well, let him come, Hallie thought, just so as cool weather comes with him. Besides, Starlin had told her about reason to hope for more sawmill work in a month or two. And cotton would be good this year. Maybe they could pick on one of the bigger farms.

"I'd make a sight better wage did I go to the mines," Star had said, but he shuddered as he spoke. "Just can't face up to it—all them dark hours under the earth, no light but from a lantern."

Hallie shuddered too at the thought of Star boarding all week in McCurtain to work at the mines, coming home on weekends to spend most of his time courting. Eventually, she supposed, Star would marry Helga and no longer live at the cabin. But that time when she would be without his strength was in the future. There would be time enough to fret over his absence later. Knowing the air would hit her face like heat from the oven on bread baking day, Hallie reluctantly left the cellar.

Necessity drove her into the sun. She had not seen Pearly for two days. If she stayed away longer, his chubby face and brown eyes might not light with recognition at the sight of her. Taking water from the kitchen bucket, she wet a rag. It would cool her face until she could stop by the stream.

"Old Dan Tucker was a mighty fine man. He washed his face in a frying pan. He combed his hair with a wagon wheel, and he died with a toothache in his heel." Singing took energy, which made her hotter, but it made her feel slightly less isolated too. Besides, she was near the swimming hole and its cool water, so she let her voice float up and into the trees as she left the path to find the spot where the creek cut into the grassy bank. Gathering her dress to her thighs and kicking off her worn-out walking shoes, Hallie dropped to the ground and eagerly slipped her burning feet and legs into the water.

Not until she was settled did she turn her head to the left and notice the circle of stones with the remains of the burned-out campfire. So, she thought, Childers ain't totally dumb. Smart enough to build his fires near the water since things got dry. Hallie turned her body to search the trees around her. Not likely he'd linger so near the path after daylight came. Well, that was his problem. She aimed to enjoy the water. Lying back to rest on the grass, she closed her eyes and imagined ice—ice all across the water—cold and hard against her skin.

The sound jerked her back to reality, the breaking of a dry branch beneath a step. Hallie's body did feel the ice. Fear made her unable to move. Childers. Childers was near, watching her.

Then the hands clapped across her arms. "Waiting for me, ain't you?"

For a second relief spread through the girl. Here at least was a familiar enemy. She struggled unsuccessfully to get up. "Get your filthy hands off me, Gid Jones!"

"Now don't fight so." He laughed, and his face was near enough hers so that his rancid breath filled her nostrils. "You'll get yourself all hot again."

"Take your hands off me." It was all she could think to say.

"After a bit, girlie. After a bit." Pinning one arm with his knee, he placed his hand just under her breast.

"My brother will kill you if you bother me." Her voice was stronger with new hope. "Or your ma. Mary sure won't hold with you doing me one speck of harm."

"Maybe." His voice was low and sickeningly sweet. "But then maybe you won't feel none like talking about the ways we find to pleasure ourselves. Ladies don't tell, you know. Or could be I'll just holt you under that there water when I'm quit with you."

Suddenly his body was stretched over hers. Even with her

eyes closed Hallie knew he was grinning. When his hand released one wrist, her lids flew open to see him working at the rope that held his pants. Scratch, she thought, go for his eyes, and her free hand shot out, fingers extended to tear at his face.

The slap was hard, and Hallie's scream mixed pain and terror. It filled her ears, and she tried to climb into the sound, to block out all else. But something interrupted, pulling her back.

"Get off her now and run. You run and you pray that I don't fill your back full of lead like you deserve."

It was a voice Hallie did not know, but for just a moment she was too weak to sit up and turn toward it.

There was the sound of Gid thrashing through the trees and there was a shot.

"I'm obliged," she said, putting her hands on the bank and forcing herself up, but the figure was disappearing into the trees. Hallie could see only a blue shirt with a tear on one shoulder.

Too weak to move, she leaned against a poplar and fought sickness. "I want my ma," she moaned, and her voice in her ears sounded like Dovie's.

Gid Jones! Vile Gid Jones had slapped her face, had touched her breasts. She was shaking uncontrollably. He would have torn off her clothing. A fierce pain shot deep within her, and she drew herself up tightly as if in an effort to ward off injury.

Maybe she would give way to hopelessness, slip down

there beneath the trees and stay unmoving until the leaves fell and covered her. "There is worse things," Ma had said of death. The truth of those words came to the girl, and took her last strength.

How could those trembling legs carry her to the cabin? But there was a sound of movement in the woods, and Hallie sprang, still whimpering, and threw herself, running, onto the trail. Panic carried her, unseeing, past the greenness as she moved toward home.

Standing at the well, Hallie drank until her hand could hold the dipper without shaking. While she had run over the path to home her mind had raced too, making three decisions. There would be no word to Mason. It was impossible to speak to her father about Gid's body, heavy over hers. Nor would she tell Starlin. There must not be a fight between her brother and Gid Jones, owner of a long knife and no conscience. It was Mary. Tomorrow she would go to Mary and beg protection from the terrible Gid. It was necessary. The stranger would not always be there. Childers! Of course! Hallie tossed water from the dipper and lowered it back to the bucket. Childers! Who else could it have been? She turned toward the trees, her eyes searching. He was out there somewhere. Childers, the mysterious young man who would not fight the great war, had saved her from Gid Jones's body and maybe from death.

When Gid was under Mary's control, Hallie planned, she would go back to the campfire near the swimming hole. There would be a trace. Maybe a footprint. Maybe the piece of cloth torn from his blue shirt. She would find something. Something to help her know him. Something to touch and say thank you to. The thought soothed her, and she was able to move calmly into the house and to begin supper.

———

THERE WAS NEWS as they gathered around the table. "High line coming." The words had moved through the village and over the mountain, coming to the cabin with Brack when he came in to eat.

"It's the gospel truth," he told the others. To Hallie the news was less important than the fact that it gave them something to talk about. No one would look at her and wonder about her quietness.

Brack was bursting with details. "They're going to string a wire from Stigler plumb over to Red Oak. Biggest stir in town—all them high-line boys coming. Boarding house likely bust at the seams."

Burch spilled his buttermilk, but no one said anything. "What for?" he demanded as Hallie wiped away the mess. "Why they fixing to put up a string?"

"For electricity," Brack explained. "Lamps that don't need no oil."

"Mr. Thomas Alva Edison," Mason commented in a rare burst of interest. "The man is a wizard, and now he will light up Lafine and Red Oak."

"Will he light up us?" Dovie asked. "Will he, Pa?" But

Mason, having finished his sweet potatoes, was going out the back door.

"No, Dovie," Star answered for their father. "Electricity ain't for us, but we'll see the high line all right."

"We can see them stringing the wire." Turner was talking loudly.

"Sure enough." Brack reached for another biscuit. "And we'll see the boys that does the work." His voice took on an exaggerated slowness. "Even Hallie might get her a feller." His words were wasted because Hallie was leaving the cabin, as her father had. She would wait again on the hitching post rock. Wait and watch for a campfire.

Dusk was settling over the hills. Shadows were lengthening and growing darker under the pines, bringing with them their companion, loneliness. "Ma," Hallie whispered. "Ma, can you hear me?" If Ma was alive, the girl thought, I'd wait until we was alone in the kitchen. She might be at the table kneading bread and me at the sideboard with dishes in a pan.

"Childers ain't bad, I'd say. You don't need to study about any harm coming to us on his account. Childers saved me from Gid. He ain't bad atall."

"We got to find him," Ma would say, wiping dough off her hands onto her apron. "It don't seem right to leave a boy like that out in the hills to face winter all hungry and cold. Tell the boys. We are beholding to find him."

"But Ma is dead," Hallie said aloud, and she kicked a stone with her toe. There was no one to talk to. Maybe if ever there was a chance, she would tell Helga. It would be awhile with Helga so caught up in courting.

Hallie was lonely, but not just for anyone. She did not welcome the sight of Ruby Willbanks waving and hurrying toward the rock. Ruby, however, never really sensitive, was far too excited to notice how Hallie felt.

"I come as soon as the table was wiped. Just walked out to leave Vida Mae the dishes." Ruby was breathing hard as she sat down. "I'm in a pickle, Hallie. A sure enough pickle and in need of advice."

"Ruby," declared Hallie with no laughter in her voice, "you been in a pickle so long, you're bound to be pickled clean through by now."

"No, now. This is a puredee serious problem." Ruby twisted at a strand of her thick hair. "Ma got me and Vida Mae work with Mrs. Bailey over to the boarding house." She jumped to her feet. "Ma is just bound sure that we both get a man amongst the high-line boys."

Hallie pulled Ruby back down on the rock. "What's got you so fired up? Likely you will." She resisted the line about Ruby's going on home now. Well, it was true. Ruby would probably capture the heart of a high-line boy as she passed him the gravy. Hallie wasn't so sure about Ruby's sister. Vida Mae had the same bony face, overly large nose, and black hair as Ruby, but the older girl's tresses were thin and limp, like Vida Mae's personality. It was Ruby who had all the spark in the family.

Plopping back down, Ruby let out a long and mournful

sigh. "Sure, there's apt to be them that takes to me. But that's where the rub comes in!" Hesitating briefly, she began to twist again at her hair. "I've got a secret I ain't ever told you."

It was enough to capture even Hallie's interest. Ruby with an untold secret. "Spill it."

"It's about the well." Ruby was almost whispering. "Higgins' well on May Day."

It was a tradition passed from woman to girl. If she looked into the huge dug well on the Higgins property on May first, looked long and with believing eyes, she would see the face of her future husband.

"So?"

"I never told it on account of him being sweet on you and all, but I got to tell it now."

"You mean Erwart? You seen Erwart Tanner's face?"

"I did." Ruby reached out for Hallie's hand. "I did sure enough. Real plain, and I'm bound to marry him. Will you hold it against me?"

"I'll not begrudge you Erwart." At another time Hallie could not have spoken without laughter. "Go right on and marry him."

"Well, there is just two things. One, I've got to convince Ma to give me time. And two, I've got to convince Erwart."

"You can. I'll just vow you can." Hallie stood up and pulled at Ruby's arm. "Do you reckon as how you ought to go on home so as not to rile your ma?"

"Maybe. Anyways I got a bunch of thinking to be done. You study on it some too, Hallie."

"I will," Hallie lied. There were far too many other things to fill her mind, and she stayed out on the rock long after the lamps went on inside the cabin.

————

THE NEXT DAY WAS FULL, the last of the okra to be picked and put up. Hallie lingered over each job, reluctant to finish because there was Mary to see. Finally, she called Watch and started out of the yard but, turning, she ran back to the kitchen for the butcher knife. With the blade held down to her side among the skirt folds, she took the trail to the Joneses' place.

Before the path widened into the yard with its immaculate rocks, Watch lay down and refused to go forward. Each Jones boy owned at least two hunting dogs, animals toughened by curses and kicks.

"All right, yeller belly," Hallie said to the sad-eyed dog. "I'll go on without you." But she no longer held the knife down. There was no sight of Mary or Shadrack. Could they be in the fields while Gid waited for her inside the cabin?

"Lands, girl, have you come to do us in?" Mary bellowed from the open door.

"No," said Hallie, stopping on the porch. She would not enter without knowing Gid's whereabouts. "No." The girl began to sob. "It's Gid. I'm fearful of Gid. He tried to hurt me."

"Child, child." Mary put a rough hand on Hallie's cheek. "Tell me now. Did that bastard have his way with you?"

Hallie dropped into a cane-bottomed chair. "He meant to. He did, but Chil . . . some stranger stopped him."

"Ain't it lucky," said Mary, "that I kept the black bastard at home to help me whilst the others went to the still!" There was a cold flatness in her words completely unlike the big powerful sounds that usually rolled from her lips.

But when she yelled, "Gid, get your lazy self out here," her voice was normal again. Then she turned back to Hallie. "Give me your knife, girl. I'm fixing to cut the bastard's heart out."

"No, I . . ." Hallie was shaking.

"Give it to me," Mary demanded, and Hallie put the knife into the outstretched hand.

Gid and Shadrack were both coming out onto the porch. "Ma," Gid began to plead. "Ma, I were just funning her. Not meaning no real harm." He was backing away toward the end of the porch.

"I'm sure enough meaning harm," Mary stepped toward him. "I'm aiming to slice you up into pieces, and I'm going to use this child's knife to do it."

"Now, might be as you ought to wait, Ma." It was a weak protest from Shadrack, completely ignored by Mary.

Gid was whimpering. "Ma, not me. You won't kill your firstborn." His face was white.

"You ain't my firstborn, not even mine neither. You belonged to some critter." She spat the accusation at him along with tobacco, taking more steps until the blade was close to his chest. "I'm thinking I might let you live, do you start to run and not stop till you come upon country ain't never seen your black bastard face. Might be I'll let you live do I never see it again my ownself, but I'd sooner kill you now and be sure of the riddance."

"My gear?" It was a question and a plea.

"No!" said Mary. "Nary a thing from my cabin, but here." With the tip of the long knife she caught Gid's cap from a nail on the porch wall. "Here, take this. It's all you'll get. I don't recollect you had even that much when they claim I birthed you."

Hallie watched Gid trudge away from the porch. At the edge of the yard, he looked back, but from the doorway Mary bellowed, "Go." Gid disappeared among the trees.

Later, Hallie took Pearly out to the bench by the smoke-house, but she was too agitated to sing to him or take much pleasure in his smiles. "Would Gid, do you think, wait out there for me?" she asked Mary when it was time to go home for fixing supper.

"He ain't plumb crazy." Mary shaded her eyes with a hand and looked toward the trees. "Something is curious, though. I walked down the trail for a piece just now, thinking about Gid. Well, I would just swear I seen something blue amongst the blackjacks. Ain't none of my boys got a blue shirt. Could it have been one of your kin, sort of watching out for you?"

Hallie too turned toward the trees. "Could be."

"I'll walk with you if you're afeared." Mary put her hand on the girl's shoulder.

"I'm obliged, Mary, but it ain't necessary. I expect I've got me someone out in them trees, someone who don't aim for no harm to come."

Moving down the trial, Hallie was aware of the sound of movement beside her—off the path, hidden in the trees. She stopped, gathered her nerve, and spoke loudly. "Come on out, Mr. Childers. I'd be pleased to thank you for what you done for me."

There was no sound from the trees. She moved closer but could see nothing among the greenness. "Well, iffen you'd rather not come out here, I'll just say thank ya, just the same."

There was the cracking of twigs, and a huge figure emerged from the undergrowth. Hallie was greatly disappointed to see Lem Crisswell. "Howdy." He took off his black felt hat.

"Hello, Lem." She was not afraid of the simple man, but she did not relish the idea of having him as a walking companion and began walking more quickly.

"You had it in your head that I were Childers, but I ain't him." He laughed and hit his hat against his leg. "I know where Childers is, though."

Now Hallie was interested. "Where?"

"Your ma died, didn't she?" He began to scratch his head.

"Yes."

"Like my pa."

Hallie thought there was little similarity between the deaths, but she nodded a yes. "Did you ever see Childers?" She was determined to get information.

"I seed him. But Ma never did." Lem was obviously proud of the fact. "Oncet he chopped wood for us. It were not long ago. I was sick with the grippe. Ma were doing the chopping, but she gived out and comed to the house. We heard the chopping, but Ma she said we had to keep inside." Lem stopped and sat down under a tree.

Hallie stopped too. "What happened when you seen him?"

Lem gave her a disgusted look. "Didn't I just tell about how Ma said we mustn't go outside? He left us a note though."

"What did it say?" She wanted to put her hands on the great shoulders and shake him, because he had begun the scratching again and seemed to have forgotten her.

"Lem! What did the note say?"

He looked up at her with surprise. "Oh, we ain't got no idea. Ma, she don't know letters. Pa did some, but my pa died."

"I know, Lem. Did you ever see Childers? I mean some other time, not when he chopped wood."

"Sure. I seen him. I'm going to town now. Ma sent me to town." He was up and gone.

Hallie walked slowly on alone. The trail was shaded from the late afternoon sun by the tall poplars growing along the riverbank. Shafts of sunlight slanted through the leaves, and spotlighted a clump of blue flowers at the base of a rock. Hallie bent quickly to gather them. Then, leaving the path, she found the burned-out campfire in its circle of stones. Kneeling, she arranged the flowers there. Taking a stick, she wrote in the ashes, "I do most surely thank you. Hallie Horton."

6

THE BALL GAME on Sunday helped push the thought of Gid Jones from the girl's mind. Because it was a rematch with Red Oak, Lafine was under pressure to uphold their earlier victory. In the Horton cabin there was even more cause for excitement. "I've got me a bet with young Erwart," said Brack at breakfast on game day. "If Lafine whips Red Oak by four points or more, I get his best boots."

"What happens were it to turn out"—Turner paused and looked down at his mush, almost unable to form the words—"the other way?"

"Ain't likely it will." Brack was grinning and turned to face Hallie at the stove. "But if by some black twist it should, I reckon I sort of told Erwart he'd be welcome to call on Hallie."

"Wow, now!" Hallie let fly with the dish towel, a direct hit on Brack's face. "You just sure enough be praying for Lafine to win by plenty. Star's not the only one hereabouts who can throw."

But through it all, Hallie noticed that Star was uncharacteristically quiet. Dressed early, Helga's red handkerchief in his pocket, he stood watching Hallie prepare a basket of food for a cold supper to eat on the way home.

With quick glances Hallie studied him. It was not like Star to be nervous. Pressure ran off her brother's back like water off Tucker's Knob. "Want some corn bread whilst it's hot?" she asked him.

He shook his head no. "Hoke Skinner claims there's a stranger been over to Stigler asking about our team."

"Well, sure. Lots of folks is interested in this game." She could see from his face that there was more, something unsaid. "What does it mean, the stranger?" She was tying corn bread in a piece of cloth.

"Could be I'm dead wrong," said the boy, and he reached for a piece of the golden bread. "Might be don't mean a thing." Then he turned and left the kitchen.

Even Mason whistled "The Band Played On" as he and Turner hitched up Doc and Red. For Hallie the pleasure was gone. It did not matter to her that her father actually laughed with the boys about Brack's wager or that the sun stayed with them on the trail, heating her back through the plaid dress and causing her to keep her head and eyes low to avoid the glare. Something troubled Star, and the puzzle of it blocked out all else.

"Machines showing up right smart in these parts," Mason said from the wagon seat as they pulled in at the ball field.

"Look!" Turner was hanging over the edge. "Can you believe it? A red one! That's not a Model T!"

"The black one's Erwart Tanner's. I bet. Ain't it grand?" Brack was standing up.

Parked along the sidelines amid the wagons were two

shiny automobiles. Near the door of the black Ford stood Erwart Tanner, Jr. with his hat in his hand. He was surrounded by admirers of the car, who were, at least for the moment, also his admirers.

Some of the boys had edged toward the red Stutz Bearcat. Because Lafine had never seen a fancy bright-colored automobile, it was more fascinating than the Ford. The driver, however, seemed too standoffish to approach. He sat there in his thick leather goggles and checkered cap with his hands still on the wheel as if undecided about staying.

As the young ones and Mason were climbing out of the wagon for a better view of the game, Ruby was scaling the side to get in. Holding on with one hand, she was brushing down her hair with the other.

"He's got a motor car. Sure enough belongs to him!" she gasped, grabbing on to Hallie's arm to pull herself over the edge.

"Yeah, it's a dandy, but who's the stranger?"

"Oh," said Ruby with a toss of her head. "Just some feller. Says he likes baseball. Shoot, forget him. He's old as your pa."

But despite Ruby's chatter, the stranger filled Hallie's thoughts until suddenly he was replaced. "Heidens ought to be here by now," she said when the game was about to start. Standing up for a better view, she shielded her eyes with her hand, searching for a glimpse of the familiar wagon.

"Reckon they won't come." Ruby's voice took on the important tone she used when giving out news. "Their fences got cut last night. Bull got out and everything. Some folks is pretty het up, him being a German and all."

"It ain't right to make them afraid to come to a game. It just ain't right." Hallie stomped her foot.

Ruby shrugged. "Never said it was, but you can't do nothing about it either. No use getting yourself all worked up."

Hallie settled back to the wagon seat. Anger boiled inside her, anger at the townspeople for hating someone just because of where he was born, anger at Ruby for enjoying the fence story, and anger at herself because Ruby was right about what she could do about it all. "Humph," she snorted in a way that reminded herself of Mary. She crossed her arms against her chest and stared at the ball field.

Excitement was rising in the crowd like swirling flood-waters. "Game's starting," Ruby commented, but she was really interested in nothing except Erwart and his automobile. After a time she had a plan. "If I was to faint, do you reckon Erwart would haul me to Stigler to the doctor?"

"Don't try it. Ain't that Doc Peters?" Hallie gestured toward a group of men. "Besides, I don't know as a body can drive a motor car barefoot, and Erwart is about to lose his boots to Brack. Bright boy like that ought to know better than to bet against Star."

Finally the game ended, Lafine twenty, Red Oak fifteen. Hallie was cheering loudly when Ruby pulled at her arm.

"Mercy," said Ruby. "Erwart's on his way over here."

But Hallie did not even turn to look in Erwart's direction.

The stranger had walked toward Star, and now the two of them were talking.

"Would you like to ride in my motorcar, Hallie?" Ruby poked Hallie until she turned to see Erwart's hopeful face staring up at her. "I'm a right good driver, sir," he added to Mason, who was now beside him.

Hallie ignored Erwart. "Pa, look!" she pointed. "What do you reckon that feller wants with Star?"

"Likely just commenting on the game. You go on and ride if you're a mind to." He was moving away from the wagon. "Believe I'll just walk over to see Star too."

"Can we all go? Can we?" Burch climbed onto the wagon wheel so that he was directly in front of Hallie's face.

"I'd not care to leave them out," Hallie said to Erwart. "And Ruby, of course. She's aiming to ride back home with us."

"It's a big motorcar," said Erwart, smiling all over himself. "And powerful too. But then, I'll be expecting to have a pretty girl sit up beside me."

"Ruby's willing to do just that, ain't you, Ruby?" Hallie laughed, but she let Erwart take her arm as she climbed down from the wagon and walked beside him to the automobile. Turner, Brack, and Burch settled into the back with Dovie on Brack's lap.

"I'll just give her a crank." Erwart's voice was full of importance. "You boys watch me now, and I might let you do the job sometime. You'd have to sure enough be careful. A feller could get injured when the crank jumps."

The backseat passengers and Ruby applauded when the engine turned over. Before Erwart took his place behind the wheel, Hallie squeezed close to Ruby, leaving a space between herself and the driver's spot. Erwart got in but wanted to talk before the actual drive. "I've got to get me a driving coat like that city man had. They're called dusters."

His words were lost on Hallie, who was looking at the field where the stranger stood talking to Mason and Star.

"Now," said Erwart, turning toward the back. "You'll needs be still." He paused to let the importance of his words sink in. "Driving an automobile takes concentration. No wiggling or tomfoolery." Ruby stifled a giggle, but Hallie needed no admonishment to be quiet.

With every turn of the tires Hallie wanted to go back, but Erwart sitting proud at the wheel, along with the "ohs" and "ahs" and the "Boy howdy," from the backseat kept her quiet for a couple of miles.

Then she spoke with a plan designed to cause Erwart to turn back. "You've got to stop, Erwart," she said. "I'm feeling poorly and best set by the air."

Erwart, full of concern, stopped immediately and helped Hallie resettle next to the door. "I'd not have you sick. Not for anything." His worried face caused Hallie guilt.

"Yeah," said Turner from the back. "It'd be plumb awful if you puked all over a motorcar."

Hallie strained for the sight of the ball field and was disappointed to see it deserted. Neither the stranger's red automobile nor Star's horse Beauty was to be seen. Only the Horton wagon waited, with Mason on the seat.

"We're obliged to you, Erwart." Hallie did not even turn toward him as she jumped out and, forgetting her illness, she ran to the wagon, pulling Ruby with her.

"Yeah," she heard Brack say. "I thank you too, but I'll still be by right soon to collect my boots."

"Hurry yourselves over here," Mason called out. "Buttercup needs milking."

Once in the wagon Hallie made herself look at Erwart to wave before she asked, "Where's Star? He go to Helga's?"

"Not knowing, couldn't say." Mason cracked the whip over Doc and Red, but Hallie noticed he held back the reins.

"Just wanted to crack the whip," Hallie whispered to Ruby. "He's mad." But she had to go on. "What the stranger want?" She studied her father's straight back.

"Just a busybody. Sticking in his nose where it ain't wanted. Like girls asking too many questions." Mason cracked the whip again.

A sickness began to grow in Hallie's stomach, reminding her of Ma's warning, "Lies come home to roost." She had no interest in the baseball or automobile talk or in the corn bread and boiled eggs she handed out to the others for the ride home. Nor did she care about Ruby's prattle concerning Erwart and how he was, Ruby believed, fixing to take notice.

Reluctant to ask Mason to drive out of his way, Ruby

jumped from the wagon at the fork where the trail led to her house. "I'll be over to see you, Hallie. You got to help me."

Hallie, who felt incapable of managing anyone's life, gave out a weary sigh, but she waved to Ruby and tried to smile.

———

WHEN THE EVENING CHORES WERE DONE, the girl sat on the rock to wait for her brother until a thunderstorm drove her inside. All night it rained. She heard the drops on the cabin roof. She heard coyotes calling to one another and the cry of a bobcat, which sent Watch into a frenzy of barking, but she did not hear the awaited step. Star did not come home. It was long after the thunder grew silent beyond the mountain that Hallie slept.

"Pa," she said when Mason came in for breakfast. "Pa, Star . . ."

Mason set the milk pitcher down hard on the table. "Leave it be, girl. Just leave it be."

Giving the plate with her untouched food a push, she moved away from the table and headed for the door.

"Set down and eat," she heard Mason bellow at someone who must have started to follow her.

Out the kitchen door, she climbed the hill behind the house and threw herself onto the damp grass. "He's stubborn and dadgum mean. Blasted old man!" She began to pull at blades of the wet greenness with a fury.

After what seemed like a long time, she saw Burch and Dovie come out to play. Then Mason and the older boys left for the fields. Brushing herself off, Hallie went back into the house to gather clothes for washing because the tubs were full of rainwater.

Working outside suited Hallie. She took wood from the shed and built a fire under the iron kettle. But her eyes were never long away from where the trail came between the pines and widened into the yard.

When the water was boiling, she shaved thin strips from the big square bar of soap and stirred them into the kettle with a stick. The familiar, strong smell of the lye was enough to make her blink, but not enough to cause the tears that ran down her cheeks.

With the washing done and hung there was nothing to do but go to the kitchen at the back of the cabin. She was determined not to run over and over to look out the window, but she did not stack the dishes as roughly as was her custom. And she listened instead of singing. She left food on the table. Might be Star would be hungry when he came, unless he had sat at the Heidens' well-spread table.

By the time the dishes were finished her mind was made up. "Burch," she called. "Dovie! Run get the rope. I'm going to ride old Doc over to see Helga."

"With no bridle?" Burch demanded. "You aiming to ride all that way with no bridle?"

"I am. I most certainly am."

"You could use Star's bridle," volunteered Dovie who had just come into the kitchen. " 'Cause he is coming up the trail."

They ran from the cabin and he was there, still in his uniform and not quite as straight as usual on the horse's back. "Run do for Beauty," Hallie said to the little ones, and she waited for her brother on the porch.

"Where you been? What in blazes is going on? What'd that feller want?" Hallie could see that Star wasn't going to stop to talk, and she followed him into the cabin.

"I'm hungry," he said, and she trotted after him to the kitchen.

"You've not been to Helga's then."

Before he spoke, he began to spread jelly on a cold corn cake. "No, to Stigler, and I'm fixing to head for Texas."

Star licked jelly from his fingers and then, straightening, he saluted. "I'm in the army now!"

"No!" Hallie stomped her foot. "No! You've got no call to go off and leave me with all this." She waved her arm to take in the cabin. "No!"

"I'll send money." His voice softened. "More than from the sawmill and steady too." He walked to the open back door and stood looking out. "Hallie, I just couldn't stay here under Pa's thumb. I'm a man now, does he know it or not."

"What happened?" She sank onto a cane-bottomed chair and put her head in her hands.

"That feller was a scout from Kansas City. Wanted to sign me up. I could of made good wages! Mighty good wages just for playing ball!" He hit his fist on the sideboard.

"So, why you fixing to go to Texas?" Her heart was pounding and she spoke loudly. Maybe he would change his mind. Anything was better than the war. A person didn't get killed playing baseball.

"It was Pa. Damn him!" Hallie had never heard Starlin sound so angry. "He was against it, and the scout said no deal without Pa's say-so. Claimed I'd not stick to it without Pa standing behind me."

"Well," said Hallie, able to raise her head. "It's a sure thing Pa will be against this army deal."

"Don't matter." Star was back at the table spreading jelly on another cake. "Don't matter one bit. The United States Army don't hold with what Pa says, not one little whit!"

"You done it to spite him." Her voice was low and lacked any feeling. "You done this thing to me just for spite against Pa." She turned her head, and he said nothing. There was only the sound of his quick chewing.

But an idea came to her. "Well, Helga then." Turning, she reached over to pull at her brother's arm. "You sure don't want to go off and leave Helga. Heidens sure need friends right now."

"It's done." There was sadness in his voice. "All settled and done when I signed that paper. The army don't allow no change of mind."

"When?" She could not look at him.

"Now," he said. "I'm fixing to change my clothes, get a thing or two, and head over to Helga's. Then come train time, I'll be on my way." He left the kitchen, but Hallie could not move.

"Your best shirt is still wet," she called to him. The

thought came to her that maybe he would wait. Maybe something would keep him from going.

"Don't need but a shirt to wear. Uncle Sam's going to be supplying me with shirts for a spell. Guess I ought to take my long johns, though. Might not be back before cold weather." He came back to the door for a moment. "Guess what? The feller at the army office says Gid Jones will be getting on the train with the Stigler bunch. Said Gid is going on to a different camp, though. Seemed to think I'd be disappointed not to be with Gid." He made an attempt at a laugh.

Hallie sat staring at the jelly spots Star had dropped on the oilcloth. So, they would be on the same train. One driven away by his mother and one by his father. She rose, got a rag, and wiped the table.

"What you doing?" she heard Burch ask Starlin, and with her fingers in her ears she ran into the back room and threw herself on her bed. She lay facedown until he came.

"Hallie." Starlin touched her shoulder. "Hallie, I've got to go now. Burch is crying on the porch and Dovie's gone off to hide somewhere."

She sat up and looked at him with cold eyes. "And you are asking me to take care of them. Fix the crying you caused." She had hurt him. It was in his face, but she did not care. "Run on and have yourself a high old time. I'll see to Burch and Dovie."

He turned to walk away, and she weakened. "I'll get Dovie," she said, and she rose to go into the kitchen. Dovie was under the table, a frequent pouting spot. She sat holding Starlin's pillow, her small face pressed into it.

"Come on out." Hallie reached in to touch the little arm. "You'd . . . we'd be mighty sorry was we to fail to say good-bye."

The three of them stood together, Hallie with an arm around each of the little ones. Dovie held the pillow until Star bent to kiss her. Then, dropping it, she threw her arms wildly around his neck. "I'm sorry to leave you with all the burden," he said when he kissed Hallie's cheek. She said nothing.

"Tell Brack to get Beauty from over to the Heidens. You can all ride him whilst I'm gone." His hand was on Burch's shoulder.

"I'll take care of him," Burch sobbed. Star gathered both the little ones to him one more time.

"Yes, sir! You two got to take care of my horse. You hear me, now?"

When he was in the saddle, Hallie ran to him. "I could fix you a lunch," she said, putting her hand on his arm. "You ain't had much."

"Thank you, no." He touched her hair. "I'll most likely have a late noon at the Heidens. The army will see to feeding me on the train. Don't fret so, Hallie. Please don't fret so." Then he was gone.

7

AND SO life without Starlin began to take shape in the cabin. Hallie missed him almost as much as she did her mother, but she comforted herself with thoughts of his homecoming. Taking out a calendar, which had once seemed unimportant, she hung it on the kitchen wall. The faces of a farmer and his children looked out at her from their cornfield. Beneath the picture were the words "Food will win the war" in big letters. Hallie marked an X across the dates since Starlin's departure. He won't be gone long, she told herself. The time will go by and he won't be gone long.

Star's leaving after their falling out seemed somehow to shake Mason from some of his indifference toward his young. "Pa reads your letters over and over," she wrote to Star. "And you won't believe this. He played a game of checkers with Turner last Sunday, and then he said I looked tired and ought to rest. Then, of all things, he fried up the taters for supper himself."

By the beginning of October, summer had allowed the days to slip through her hot hands, and autumn was moving in, ready to add touches of color to the trees. In the hills rattlesnakes came out on the rocks to sun themselves as if trying to store up warmth for the days ahead.

Finally, a suitable master having been found, school was ready to begin. Hallie had expected to feel glad to have the young ones out of the cabin, but on the night before classes started the sunset made her unbearably lonely. What was she to do all day alone? In another month little Pearly would keep her busy. "Cow's milk will do him by then," Mary had said, and she helped Hallie find bottles in the Wish Book.

Mason had surprised Hallie again by seeming to be anxious to have Pearly home. "Baby will liven things up around here," he had said, "give us less time to study on what we've lost," and he gladly supplied the money for the catalog order.

There was nothing for Hallie to do now but wait. Filling the children's lunch buckets in the morning, Hallie felt restless. The beginning of school had always been exciting. What was there for her now? She tried to forget the lonely ache inside by paying special attention to Dovie's lunch. For the boys it did not matter how the food looked, but Hallie determined that for Dovie the meal should be pretty. She remembered how as a little girl she had longed for food that would make someone envious. Ma's cooking had been good, but leftovers had gone into lunch buckets. The smaller girls always made a production of taking each item from their buckets and holding it up for the others to see. At least they did if their lunch was enviable. Boiled eggs were good enough for the others, but for Dovie there would be two deviled eggs, a pretty green pepper, and some plum jelly in a jar to spread on her bread.

"It ain't fair how boys got to set away on one side and

girls on the other," Dovie complained at breakfast. "Burch will most likely get to be by Turner and me over there by myself."

"I won't be in them primary seats," Turner corrected her. "I finished two grades last term."

"You'll be by a nice little girl." Hallie reached for Dovie and gave her a hug. "You're going to school at a younger age than any of the rest of us did. That's on account of the master saying you're smart, and you're brave too."

It was true. Dovie had spunk, a necessary commodity and one that Hallie lacked. If Dovie was me, Hallie thought, she sure wouldn't be too fearful to go over to the store today and watch Proc Maylor's trial. Helga can't go with me. The Heidens, sending their hired man for supplies, never went into town now. Well, maybe Ruby could slip away from the boardinghouse, but probably if Hallie went, she would have to be brave enough to go alone.

"We are taking the wagon to town," she announced to the others as she cleared the table. "I'll drive you by the school then go on over to watch the trial."

"They'll hang old Proc for killing Sim Lawrence. That's for sure," Turner predicted.

"You just turn your mind to learning and leave hanging to the judge." Hallie's words sounded in her own ears like those of her mother.

On the road in front of the school, the ice wagon was stopping at the Atkinses' house. Four or five children were already in pursuit, and the Hortons jumped out to join them. Ice deliveries were an occasion. Previously the wagon had made a stop only at the store. But now that more homes contained ice boxes, home deliveries had begun. It was a great excitement for the children, who would catch up with the wagon just in time to be on hand when blocks were chipped off. They were allowed to take the tiny pieces that fell away from the ice pick.

Hallie, watching the children putting out their hands to grab thin pieces of ice, felt sorry to have left childhood's pleasures behind. "Don't you forget school," she cautioned and drove the wagon around the laughing children.

The boardinghouse—big, white, and containing a modern toilet—had always been interesting to Hallie, who had longed for a reason to go inside. But this morning she had no nerve to do so and stood outside planning what to do. At the kitchen door there might be a chance to see Ruby without encountering Mrs. Bailey's notoriously sharp tongue. Sure enough, just as Hallie rounded the edge of the house, Ruby came out with scraps for the dog.

"Ruby," she called, relieved.

"Lands, girl." Ruby ran to her. "I ain't seen you in a coon's age. Don't you never come to town no more?" Suddenly Ruby's face changed, and she pulled at her hair. "Star? Nothing ain't happened to Star?"

"No." Hallie felt irritated. How could Ruby think anything would happen to Star. It wouldn't, not ever. "He's still in training in Texas. We get letters. I just come to see you. Thought maybe you could slip off with me and go to Proc Maylor's trial."

Ruby shook her head in despair. "Ain't possible. Mrs. Bailey would skin me, sure. Oh, lands, I wish I could, not so much on account of the trial as to see Erwart at the store. I don't hardly ever get to go over there."

Hallie laughed. "You ain't fell for no high-line boy, then, I reckon."

Ruby was shocked. "Oh, Hallie, ain't you heard? They ain't high-line boys atall. It's on account of the war. There ain't enough men for such work. They is all prisoners from McAlister Prison. Ain't it something?"

"Sure enough? You scared to death?"

"Not a bit." Ruby tossed her hair. "They is all polite to us ladies. Have to be. There's guards and all. And guess what? Number fifteen seems to be getting sweet on Vida Mae. Ma says like as not he didn't do nothing real bad or either he is reformed and all."

"Well, that's sensible." Hallie was laughing.

"Mercy, I've got to scat." Ruby turned to run. "But Hallie, iffen you see Erwart, don't smile at him. He's just got to quit hankering after you."

"I won't smile. Might not even go over there without you for company." She waved and walked slowly back to the wagon, but once on the seat, she turned the horses toward the store. "Be brave," she said aloud. The building would be crowded. Maybe she could just slip in, just stand near the door.

But her plan was ruined. "Clear the door. Move on down. There's places on the benches," Mrs. Tanner directed the crowd, and Hallie felt too timid to protest. Settling quickly on the end of a row, she tried to forget her self-consciousness by casting shy looks toward the front of the store at Proctor Maylor, who was on trial for the murder of Sim Lawrence. Dad Henderson, Justice of the Peace, was nodding behind a makeshift desk. He was a man of considerable age, who was inclined to wet his pants if the trial took long. Last year when the now deceased Sim Lawrence had shot Theodore Riley over a card game, Dad had declared Sim innocent of murder on the grounds that Theodore was a drunken ne'er-do-well who needed shooting and Sim was an upright citizen.

Now Dad roused himself for the verdict. "Not guilty," he muttered.

"But Your Honor," the prosecutor protested. "The trial isn't over."

Dad replied, but his voice was too soft for Hallie, even near the front as she was, to catch much of what he said.

"Speak up, Dad," a man yelled. "We can't hear a thing."

Justice Henderson stood. He was a short man, who seemed even smaller leaning on the desk. "I said not guilty. Proc here is an upstanding man, cornerstone of Lafine. Sim Lawrence was a card-playing hothead with a bad reputation for gun play. Court dismissed."

There were cheers from the crowd. Proctor and his brothers gathered around to shake Dad's hand. Hallie wondered if the justice had remained dry due to the brevity of the trial, but she could not see.

She was smiling over Dad's verdict, thinking how it would be something to write to Star about, and she did not notice at first that her way was being blocked as she moved toward the door.

"Ain't you one of that Horton bunch?" There was whiskey on Elton Holmes's breath. Hallie stepped back from the smell and from the man.

Looking around for a friendly face to call to, Hallie said nothing. "Sure she is," Roscoe Williams commented from beside Elton, his voice full of scorn. "Her brother ain't here now to talk pretty words."

"He's gone to war," said Hallie. Maybe they would be satisfied, not wanting to bother a soldier's sister.

"Heard," said Elton. "Never figured a German lover would want to fight."

Hallie moved to walk away, but Roscoe stepped to block her again. "Me and Elton here just been talking as to how we oughta get a bunch of fellers, hunt down that slacker that's hiding up around your place." He looked at his friend for confirmation.

"Yeah." Elton hitched up his pants. "Yeller belly not willing to fight oughta be shot down like a coyote."

Hallie wanted to ask why the two men themselves were not in the army, but she dared not.

"You seen that damn slacker?" Roscoe took a step toward her.

"No." It was true. There had not been even a sign of a campfire for several days. "There ain't been no trace for quite a spell now."

"He better be gone iffen he knows what's good for him! He just better be." Elton was pounding one fist into his other hand. He leaned over, his hideous breath again in Hallie's face. "And you, young missy, you better watch who you spend your time with."

"It ain't safe to have Germans for friends, huh?" Roscoe laughed and slapped Elton's back.

They were moving away then, and Hallie sank back down on the bench, ignoring the people moving around her. She was shaking with fear. It had been foolish of her to come here alone. Ma had been right to want to keep her family in the hills away from the town. "You get around people, trouble is bound to come along," she had often said, and she had told how her own father, Hallie's grandfather, had been falsely accused of stealing when he made a trip into town.

Listening to her mother's warning, Hallie had protested. In those days, she had loved trips to town, seeing people, taking in the smell of new cloth in the store. Now I know, Ma, she thought, and she gripped the back of the wooden bench.

She would miss the excitement of going to town. It had eased her missing Star some to have people asking about him and asking her to send him good wishes. But, she determined, it had to be done. The young ones would go to school, but they would stay away from Lafine as much as possible. It was the thing to do until Star came home.

When her legs felt stronger, the girl moved toward the door, anxious to drive her wagon back into the hills where she belonged. Young Erwart was holding the door for exiting spectators. "Hallie," he said, smiling broadly.

"Get the broom, son," called Mrs. Tanner. "Store needs sweeping."

"Don't pay Ma no mind," he whispered.

His voice was sad, and Hallie had no wish to make him feel worse. Still, the truth was waiting to be told. She had little strength left for thinking of gentle ways to tell it. She kept her head bent. "Erwart, there just plain ain't no use for you to think of courting me."

He made no sound, and she plunged on quickly. "I'm just plain out not the girl for you." She raised her head but did not meet his eyes. "Maybe you ought to give Ruby some thought." She moved away. Then without looking she called back over her shoulder. "Don't give Brack your boots. It weren't a proper bet."

In the wagon, she urged Doc and Red on. Back in the hills she would go over to hold Pearly. Maybe she would take him home with her for just an hour or so to the cabin. It was time for him to see his home. She would spend the winter in the cabin. She would mark the calendar and wait for Star to come home.

It would have been good just to forget the trouble thickening in town, but then the wagon was at the Heiden turnoff, just before the road began to climb up into the hills. Hallie pulled back on the reins and looked long down the trail. She could see the smoke from the Heidens' chimney. She could picture Helga in the kitchen. Could she stay all winter by her fire and refuse to worry about Helga, whose sweet face stayed in her mind? Could she forget about Mr. Heiden and his gentle ways? And there was Childers. Hallie remembered his voice, his blue shirt moving into the trees after he had driven away the horrible Gid. He was out there among the pines. Would Elton and Roscoe find him? Should she not try to help her defender?

She urged the horses on, but a great chill came to her. It was all so fearsome. Ma had left her. Star had left her. There was no one to help her, and Hallie was powerfully afraid, knowing somehow that she would be unable to hide from the hatred growing in the town.

8

DECISION TIME CAME to Hallie that very day, even before twilight shadows touched the cabin. By the time the children came over the hills from school, she had returned Pearly to Mary's and cooked up a big pot of beans. Watch's happy barks announced their arrival. Dovie ran into the kitchen. "I wrote my name. "D-O-V-I-E," she spelled it out.

"We run races at noontime," Burch interrupted. "You want to watch me practice after supper?"

But when the older boys came in with their news, Hallie could no longer listen to the younger children's prattle.

"We seen two guys with guns," Turner told her. "Said they was looking for Childers."

"Elton Holmes and Roscoe Williams was on the trail," added Brack as he lifted the bean pot lid for a long whiff. "Dang fools like that out with guns. Makes me nervous. Where's Pa? Could get hisself shot out in them trees."

"He's in the barn." She waved her spoon at them. "Go out and tell him about the guns." Hallie wanted a minute before supper, a minute to think. They will kill Childers. Shoot him like a dog. Visions of a blood-splattered blue shirt filled her mind. Sinking into a chair, she leaned against the table for a few minutes.

"Stay out of other folks' business," she could imagine her mother would say. But then, hadn't Ma always believed in repaying people when you were beholden to them?

Hallie stood, walked to the big stove, and began to ladle cups of juicy brown beans into bowls. Her movements were sure, determined. Her mind was made up. God, she prayed. Don't let them find him now. Give me one more day. Just one more day.

Dawn found the girl awake, planning and waiting. "Hurry," she said to the young ones as she woke them the next morning. "You got to allow time for walking today." At breakfast too, she urged them to eat quickly. "It sure does rile a schoolmaster when his scholars are late."

Burch couldn't find his shoe, but finally Hallie retrieved it from under the kitchen table. At last, lunch buckets in hand, they streamed out the door. Hallie followed and stood watching as they left the clearing. Pa, already off in the fields, had taken a lunch. It was perfect. There would be no one to wonder over Hallie's absence. Quickly she untied her apron and threw it over the well bucket. "Come," she called to Watch. "Come on quick else I might lose my nerve."

She kept to the trail until it forked off in two directions to town or to the Jones place. There she left the wagon road and began to pick a path, up, up to the Crisswells'. "I seed him. Sure I seed him." Lem's words kept going through her mind. "He left a note." Maybe Lem really could lead her to Childers, or maybe the note would contain a clue.

Even Watch was tired before the tiny cabin came into

view. Why did old Mrs. Crisswell continue to live so far up here with not even a wagon road and only Lem to help her? But then, where could she go? Hallie sat down on a moss-covered rock to rest and collect herself before going closer.

The Crisswell dogs were more social than their owners. Evidently well acquainted with Watch, they gave friendly barks as he approached. Old Mrs. Crisswell came to the door and stepped out onto the big rock that served as a porch.

"Hello," she yelled to the woman. "It's Hallie, Mason Horton's girl. I've come to talk to you."

"Goodness sakes, child," called Mrs. Crisswell. "Don't be settling yourself out on a rock then. Get on in here." She stepped back inside holding the door for Hallie. "I don't hardly ever get no company," she told the approaching girl. "Come in, child. Come in."

Leaving the bright sun, Hallie could see nothing for a moment in the tiny, dark kitchen. "Take a chair." Mrs. Crisswell pulled one away from the table. "I'll fetch you a cup of water."

The woman moved quickly in spite of her age and was back with the drink before Hallie had time to think of what she would say. "Thank you." Hallie drank the water and then stared at the cup as if trying to memorize it as the hostess took a chair for herself.

"I ain't seen none of you folks since your ma died." She reached out a worn hand and touched the girl. "I'm right sorry. She were kind to me when I lost my man."

"Thank you." Hallie knew she couldn't limit her conversation to those two words. "Well," she began to speak rapidly. "I've come to ask a favor."

"Ask it." Mrs. Crisswell patted at the gray knot of hair fastened at the back of her head.

"I'm trying"—Hallie studied the cup some more—"to find out about the feller Childers that was camping around these parts for a spell."

"He were helpful to us." There was an edge of mistrust in the old woman's voice. "I'd not want to bring trouble onto him."

"Oh, no," Hallie looked up now. "Me neither. Not ever. He saved me from serious hurt by Gid Jones."

"Why you asking now? We ain't seen no sign of him for a few days. I reckon that boy is gone."

"Lem said Childers wrote you a note." Hallie studied the lined face and sharp gray eyes.

"That youngun. He does go on. He been hanging around your place?"

"I met him on the trail."

"Well, that's good. I'd not want him a bothering none. Lem" she hesitated—"he ain't quite right." She motioned toward her head.

"But the note." Hallie was stronger now, more determined. "Was there one?"

"Well, yes." Mrs. Crisswell was looking around the room. "Let me see. Where did I put that? I were of a mind to save it." She stood up. "Thought might be someone would come along to tell what it were about."

Hallie said nothing, but watched closely as the woman moved to the pie safe and took out an old tin. She removed the lid but replaced it immediately.

"Oh, lands. I don't reckon I can find it." She came back toward the chair.

"Maybe it's in the other room." Hallie pointed toward the door and stood up. She couldn't let the woman stop searching.

There was a noise, and Lem's frame filled the doorway. He stood there, not moving, staring at Hallie.

"Come on in, boy," said his mother. "We just got us some company."

Lem smiled and lumbered into the room.

"I'm a-looking for that note." Mrs. Crisswell lifted the edge of the oilcloth from the table. "The one that feller left."

"Shucks," said Lem as he moved to the water bucket and took out the dipper. "I know where it's at."

"Where?" Hallie wanted to scream, but Lem was drinking, and Mrs. Crisswell, obviously doubting the truth of his words, continued to search under bowls and plates.

"You put it in Pa's Bible." There was exasperation in Lem's words.

His mother threw up her hands in surprise. "It's a fact! I recollect now." She disappeared into the other room.

Hallie tried to think of something to say to Lem, who stared at her from across the kitchen, but Mrs. Crisswell was back before anything came to her.

She carried a big brown Bible and was leafing through it

as she walked. She sat down at the table. "Here." She handed a piece of folded paper to Hallie. It was old paper, and it cracked where the fold had been. Hallie began to read and then stopped. "It's a letter from someone named Nell."

"Well, sakes, that ain't it. Nell were Columbus's sister. She's dead too now. Let me think. How long has Nell been dead? Mrs. Crisswell stopped looking through the Bible and stared at the floor. "I can't seem to remember hardly nothing nowadays."

Hallie wanted to shout that she did not care when Nell had departed, but she held herself back. "The note," she said. "Do you think it's really in there?"

The woman began to turn again. "I 'spect this is it." She passed a piece of torn tablet paper to Hallie, whose hand shook as she took it.

"Please, ma'am," she read aloud. "You have nothing to fear from me. I knocked at your door, but you did not come. I would be glad to chop more wood for you in exchange for some hot biscuits."

"Ain't that a shame. That boy hungry for hot bread. I wished I'd knowed."

Hallie was disappointed. The note held no hint that would help her find Childers.

"I know where he's at," Lem announced.

"You do?" Hallie was excited.

"Now, boy," the woman put in, "don't go telling tales that ain't so."

"No, Ma. It ain't no tale. I seen Childers just last night."

He dropped his head. "I weren't going to tell you 'cause I afeared you'd make me go back up there where he was."

Hallie moved to the edge of her chair, staring into Lem's face. Was he telling the truth? Surely his mother could tell.

"Why'd you think I'd send you back?"

Lem did not look up, did not answer.

"Lem?" His mother's voice was sharp. "Answer me."

"You couldn't climb up there, Ma." He inclined his head in the direction where the land went up even more. "I didn't want you to send me back." He paused, looking at his hands. "I think Childers, he's like Pa."

Hallie had no idea what Lem meant, but his mother seemed to follow his thinking. "Dead? What makes you figure him for dead? Speak up, boy."

"Just a-laying there, not moving at all. I walked right close and looked. He's like Pa."

Mrs. Crisswell made a clucking noise with her tongue. "Poor boy. Sure could chop wood good."

Hallie stood up, holding for a second to the back of the chair. "Thank you." She turned toward the door.

"Don't rush off. We don't never get no company."

Hallie tried to smile at the woman, but she did not linger. Down the trail just a bit, she dropped to a rock. Was it true? Had she waited too late? Was her rescuer really dead out there in the trees, left for varmints to feed on? Lem's mother seemed to believe him, but Hallie wouldn't let herself accept it. Lem had a simple mind. Maybe he had made the whole thing up. She stood, cupped her hands, and shouted, "Mr. Childers, are you out there?"

"He can't hear you." Lem was behind her. "He can't hear nothing no more."

"Can you show me, Lem?"

"I could if I was a mind to." There was pride in his voice.

"Please, Lem, please."

Without an answer he turned and walked away from her. Watching, Hallie thought of shouting her question again. Maybe she could think of some bribe to offer him? "Wait."

He turned back to face her. "You coming or just staring?"

"I'm coming. I'm coming, Lem. You bet I am." She moved to join him, but he forged ahead, and she had to run.

Lem's legs were long, and he stayed well ahead of her. Sometimes a tree or rock blocked her view, forcing her to follow the sound of breaking underbrush and dried leaves. Then suddenly he stopped.

Hallie saw him raise his arm to point off to his left. "I ain't going over there. Pa got dead, but I didn't like to see him." He shifted his body to the other direction and was gone.

Pine trees were thick in front of her. Straining forward she tried to see. She could push herself through the thicket. Without Lem to break the trail it wouldn't be easy. Fear made her feel cold and weak. Maybe she should go home. After all, she was no more eager to face a dead man than

Lem had been. Still, she moved forward, picking her way with caution and dread. Then the trees thinned out, and she saw him, a hunched form lying motionless on a blanket.

Hallie stood still, holding to a leafless limb, and cleared her throat. "Mr. Childers," she said softly. Then louder, "Mr. Childers, do you hear me?"

On tiptoe she inched forward across the flat rock where he lay. Her arms were drawn close to her body, head down. It seemed to take a very long time to cover the mossy surface of the boulder. Then beside him, she looked down on his unshaven face and closed eyes. Still there was no sign of life.

Crouching, she forced out a hand and rested it on his chest. Yes! Yes, there was movement. "You're not dead," she murmured. "You're not dead at all," but the form did not answer.

A redness was visible on his face, and a touch proved what Hallie suspected. "Fever. You're awful hot." Her eyes searched for a container to carry water, but there was none. "The stream's close," she told him. "Maybe I ought to just drag you over there."

She gathered the edges of the blanket, keeping her eyes on the man. "I'm pretty strong, all that hoeing, I reckon, but still it's lucky you're here on this rock." She glanced around her. "Don't know as I could of got you through the trees."

Hallie pulled hard on the blanket, inching along the smooth surface. Once during the struggle, the burden groaned. She tensed, then relaxed. "It's good, I guess. At least I know you're still alive." She studied his face. What if he opened his eyes and demanded to know why some girl was pulling him over rocks to the creek? Would he think she planned to drown him?

She pulled again, and finally they were at the stream's edge. Hallie dropped beside him, eased his head into her lap, and scooped her hand into the water to dampen his forehead and lips. He wore the same torn blue shirt. With shaking fingers, she unbuttoned it. Wouldn't Ruby have a story to tell could she see this, Hallie thought as she splashed water across the burning chest.

Then his eyes were open and she was looking into them, blue as the shirt and cloudy with pain.

"It's me, Hallie," she said, sure suddenly that he would know her. "I left you a note, but that weren't enough. I come to help you."

His lips moved in a fragile smile. "Johnny Childers," he whispered. "Pleased to meet you." His eyes closed again.

"More water. You need more water." She leaned to reach the stream again, then moved her cupped hand quickly to his dry lips. "Drink," she pleaded. "Wake up and drink." The water trickled through her fingers into his mouth.

He coughed and his eyes opened again. She had to get information. "What's ailing you?" He said nothing, and she tried again. "How long you been like this?"

"Infection. My leg."

Hallie looked down and noticed for the first time that the leg of his pants had been torn away to reveal an angry sore.

"Fell," he explained. "Cut it on sharp rock. Last I

remember it was night, and I was trying to get to water." Shaking, he reached for her hand. "More, please."

When he had drunk again from her hand, she eased his head back down onto the blanket. "I'll get you help," she said, but then reality pushed its way into her mind, and she was afraid. "We got to be so careful. Oh, we sure got to be careful."

She lifted his head for another drink, and this time she felt how the sun heated the matted curls of his thick dark hair. "Too hot for a man with a fever. I ought to get you to the shade." She stood and began to pull again at the blanket.

"Wait. If you help me up, I might be able to walk." But even his voice was weak.

Suddenly, in the middle of the struggle to help him, Hallie felt embarrassed to have her arms tightly around his waist and to have him leaning heavily on her. "Oh, Lord," she said, "we sure can't get down no mountain this way."

"Am I hurting you?" His blue eyes were full of concern, and Hallie looked away from them quickly.

"No. Here, just a few more steps to shade." Don't go acting crazy, she told herself. This here is serious business.

"There," she said, when he was settled under a big cottonwood with the blanket as a pillow beneath his head. "I'll rush so fast and be back with food and maybe medicine." Her mind was racing. What medicine? How could she get help for him without putting him in danger? She had to take him off the mountain, but if word got out, a hanging party would find him before any medicine could help.

His eyes were closed again, and she stood openly staring at him for a minute before tearing off through the trees. As she moved, she tried to plan. There was of course only one place she could take Johnny.

She would get Beauty. The hills rose gently enough for the horse's sure feet to hold. Pa wouldn't be in the cabin. She would find something to feed the man. What would she do about medicine? She was crashing down the hillside, breaking bare limbs and sending pine cones flying.

"Whoa," she said aloud. You got to be able to find your way back. Look around. Find some landmarks. She glanced back toward where she had started. There's that big rock with the point. Now go straight down to that dead tree. From the tree, she could look below and see the Crisswells' place. She knew the way home, and she moved quickly until all at once there was a form before her.

Hallie stopped suddenly, her hand flying to her mouth. "Lem," she shrieked. "You scared the dickens out of me."

"You been up there with him?"

"Yes." Her heart beat fast. "You sure was right, Lem. He's dead. Just dead as a doornail. Well, I'm going to go home, get a shovel, and bury him."

"We got a shovel," Lem said.

"Well, I reckon I'll just go on to my place." She made her voice serious, full of warning. "Lem, I wouldn't go up around there for a spell. Childers has got spots all over him. Must of died of some kind of pox, might be sort of hanging in the air."

"Huh?" His face was twisted with confusion. "Huh?"

"The disease," she spoke slowly, "you know, the thing that killed him. It might be in the air up in there. You could get it, and likely you'd die too."

"No."

He was afraid, and Hallie felt sorry. But she continued, "I reckon, just to be safe, you ought to stay just real close to your place the rest of this day. Still"—she paused—"your ma might say that you should help me bury Childers. It might be best not to tell your ma," she said, but it was to his back. Lem was moving quickly toward his home.

Watch, who had been off with the Crisswells' dogs, ran to her. "If you're coming with me, you best get ready to move," she told him, and she began to race toward home.

Pa was, as she had predicted, still in the field. In the kitchen, she stood still for just a minute, listening. Everything was quiet in the cabin. The stillness made her uneasy. Quickly she gathered cold biscuits, buttermilk in a jar, a cup for water, a spoon, and a pear left to ripen on the windowsill. Then she thought of needing a knife. The fruit would be easier for a sick man to eat cut into thin slices. She reached for a small paring knife but put it down to take the big butcher knife. Might need defense, she told herself, for me or for Childers.

She wet her thumb and ran it along the knife blade, testing its sharpness. It still held an edge, and Hallie nodded her head with satisfaction. She had known it would be so. Her ma's knives were always sharp. Closing her eyes, she saw her ma sitting at the kitchen table, whetstone in her hand. "Child," she had said, spitting on the stone and moving the steel blade in small circles, "a dull knife is worthless."

"Thanks, ma," she whispered into the empty cabin, and the sense of her mother's presence gave her courage. She felt the knife blade again. Could you use that on a real man, even one like Elton or Jesse? It was a question she hoped never to have to answer.

All right. The food would give him some strength until she could do better, but what about the medicine? She looked helplessly around the kitchen. There was nothing. Mary. She would have to go to Mary again for help.

With the food and knife in a flour sack, Hallie rushed from the cabin and out to the barn. Now there was no hesitation in her step or in her purpose. Her ma was with her. "Like a woman grown, Ma." She panted, remembering what her mother had said before she died, "Like a woman grown."

The sun was directly overhead, noontime. "We got to hurry," she told the horse as she put on the saddle.

Mary was on the porch cutting her toenails again, as she had been on the day Hallie brought Pearly. The sight had been a thing of dread then. Now the presence of the bulky figure was a comfort.

"Think the little fellow's been looking for you," the woman said as she followed Hallie into the cabin. Pearly was lying on a pallet on the floor. His eyes were on Hallie, and he was smiling.

Unable to ignore him, the girl swept the baby swiftly into

her arms and kissed his soft cheek. "Oh, Mary," she gasped. "I got sickness to deal with. Fever and a terrible festered sore. He even passed out. What can I do?"

The woman was moving toward the back room. "Lands, girl, let me get the baby basket and my medicine."

Hallie shifted Pearly so as to reach out a hand to touch the big arm. "Mary, can you just tell me? Maybe give me the medicine?" Hallie knew her voice sounded strange, and Mary looked closely at her.

"What is it, child? What's got you all stewed up?"

Hallie searched for something to say, some believable story. She had planned to say it was Brack who was sick, but now she could see holes in that approach. "I've got a friend, Mary. One that is real skittery. I'm grateful, you being willing to help, but maybe you'd better just guide me as to what to do."

"Girl, it troubles me to see you fretting. I'd not want to see you in some muddle and me not helping."

"You'll help if you tell me what to do."

Mary walked to a shelf and took a bottle containing crushed leaves. "The first thing, I reckon, is a poultice to fight the pus. This friend at your place?"

Hallie was putting down little Pearly and had her back turned to Mary. It was easier that way. "No. I got to take the medicine to him."

"Well," said Mary. "You put the leaves in this here little bag and soak them for a time in boiling water. Then drain off the water and lay the poultice on the sore. Mind you don't burn yourself or the sick one."

"I'll be careful."

From the shelf Mary took an envelope. "There's just a bit of this fever powder left. Mix it with water. Might be enough to ease the sickness some."

Hallie opened the flour sack to add the medicine and was aware that Mary was looking down at the contents. "Thank you, Mary. I got to run."

"I wish you would tell me what you're up to."

"Don't worry about me." Without thinking, Hallie gave Mary a quick hug. When she stepped back, a little embarrassed, she saw that there were tears in the woman's eyes.

"Bless you, child, just bless your heart."

Hallie was out the door, flying down the steps to Beauty's back and urging the horse up the autumn trail to the cutoff.

The climb to the Crisswells' took forever. Sometimes the way had to be cleared for the horse. Beauty was obedient and surefooted, but still they moved slowly. The girl fretted with each step.

Near his house, Hallie began to worry about Lem. He could be watching you, she warned herself, and she looked frequently over her shoulder. She hoped she had made him believe Childers was dead. Lem went into the store sometimes. Maybe he would repeat the story there. Then a new fear came to her. Maybe Childers really would be dead when she got back.

Praying, she climbed on, marking the fallen tree and then the big rock. He was still there when she broke into the clearing and jumped from the horse. "Johnny," she called, and felt no shyness about using the first name. "Johnny, I'm back." Still there was no sound, no movement. Hallie stopped, fear making her move gently toward the form. "If he's dead," she whispered, "I couldn't stand it. I just plain could not stand it."

9

THEN HER HAND was on his bare chest and was being lifted and lowered slowly with his breathing. "You ain't dead," she said aloud. "Oh, I'm so glad you ain't dead."

"Me too," he said as his eyelids fluttered open. Hallie had to bend close to hear the words.

She took items from the bag to set out on the rock. "We'll start with the buttermilk. We got plenty. Since Ma died Mrs. Atkins don't hardly buy none from us." It was a silly thing to have told him. Don't rattle on, she scolded herself as she lifted his head to her knee and held the jar to his lips.

With a spoon she stirred Mary's powder into a cup of water from the river. "Now, I reckon this is bitter. Don't spit it out. I'll give you buttermilk right after."

"You're a good nurse," he said after the medicine and the milk.

Hallie felt warm with pleasure. She would see him strong and well again. Suddenly it meant everything to her. "Could you eat some pear was I to slice it right thin?"

He was sleeping again. Glancing timidly at the head resting on her lap, she studied the dark hair, strong chin, and lips curved peacefully in sleep. Her fingers touched the wooden knife handle. There was no doubt now. "I'd use this to protect you," she whispered. "I promise." When the pear was peeled, she held a thin slice to his lips. "Here, now." She roused him. "You've got to have food."

Obediently, the lips parted, and Hallie began to put in the fruit, one tiny slice at a time, but in the distance she heard the cry of a wild turkey. "Meat would be good, but this pear beats nothing."

"Tastes good."

"It's the last from our tree. The kids finished off most of them, but I did put up some." There was no time for talk about pear trees when important things had to be decided. She spoke with determination. "We got to get you out of here before they come to get you."

He shook his head slowly from side to side. "I'm not running anymore. I was coming down when I got hurt. Thought I'd wait until my leg was better."

She bit at her lip. "They won't give you no time to say you're willing to fight in the war."

He stirred, using his elbow to lift himself slightly. "No, I won't fight. Not in this war, but I won't hide anymore either. Civil disobedience. Henry David Thoreau went to jail for it. I will too."

"I don't know that Thoreau fellow, but I sure know Elton and Roscoe. They'd sooner shoot you than look at you. Wouldn't give you no chance to live long enough for jail."

"What if . . ." He stopped to cough, and Hallie pressed him gently back against her lap.

"You rest. I got to think." His eyes closed, but she peered

into the trees. If Roscoe and Elton should suddenly break through the pines, Johnny would be shot or hanged. There would be no talking. She shivered.

Whether he liked it or not, hiding would still be necessary until he was away from Lafine.

I'll let him rest just a few minutes more, she thought. For the first time that morning, Hallie allowed herself to relax a little. Her thoughts quieted, slowed, keeping pace with the slow rising and falling of Childers's chest as he breathed. Hallie looked around then at the hills, her hills. A breeze sprang up from across the Mountain Fork, riffling the surface of the clear water as it made its way toward them.

For a time she sat quietly. Somewhere across the mountain, in the next hollow, the sound of an ax pounded steadily. Her senses sharper now, she leaned into the wind, listening. Far off to the north, across the creek, she could hear wagon wheels screeching along the road to town. A sudden realization made her draw her breath sharply. "People are in these hills." She touched Childers's forehead gently. "Oh, Johnny, we got to go soon, and we got to be so watchful."

Carefully she shook his shoulder until he woke. She thought his eyes looked better, and he moved his head with more strength. Maybe the medicine and the small amount of food had already helped. "Try to get something more down," she said and broke the bread into tiny bits to dip into the remaining buttermilk. Then, with his head still resting against her lap, she spooned the mixture into his mouth.

"Good bread. It's something I've not tasted for a time."

"My ma could make the best bread, but she died." Hallie's words reminded herself of Lem talking about his pa. Johnny would think she wasn't right in the head.

"That's rough," he said. "Real rough on a kid."

Her heart was warmed by the sympathetic words, but she wanted to protest the kid part. "I'm pretty well grown," she said. "Near sixteen."

"Oh," he said. "Excuse me."

Hallie had the feeling that he would have smiled had he been stronger. She did not want to be made fun of. She knew serious facts. "There's fellows in town think of you as a slacker. They wouldn't give you no chance to say nothing if they was to run across you." She eased his head from her lap and walked to the edge of the clearing, listening.

"My aunt lives in Talequah. I've got friends in Tulsa too. They'd come if I asked."

She knelt beside him. Searching his face, she found the courage to ask. "Why won't you go?" she asked. "Why you so all-fired determined not to fight? Are you afraid?"

Despite the smile there was a sadness in his face. "Yes, Hallie. I'm afraid. Any man not afraid of war is a fool, but I'd go if I could feel this fight was right. I'd be willing to die, I think, if I could believe this was really the war to end all wars, like they say."

"You've studied about it all?" she asked. "You've been to school lots, I suspect."

He nodded. "I've been to school. Over to the University of Oklahoma, but I learned about war from my aunt Abby."

He managed a slight laugh. "Feistiest little woman alive. She brought me up. My father died in the Spanish-American War, and my mother didn't live long after. Aunt Abby didn't believe in that war either. Thought it had more to do with acquiring possessions than it did with freeing Cuba. The Civil War, though, she says she would have been glad to fight in that one, against slavery and for the union."

"Women don't have to fight," said Hallie. "Reckon we're lucky. I'm not brave like my brother."

He smiled at her. "I don't think that's true, Hallie. You'd fight. You'd fight to save anyone you love."

She wondered if he had heard her promise to protect him, and her face grew red. Well, it was true. She touched the knife. She would fight if she had to. "We got to plan. I have friends will hide you from them idiots in town until we can get you away, but we got to get you down from here on a horse. Then into my pa's wagon."

"How do you know these people will take me in?"

Hallie picked up a tiny twig and sat snapping it into pieces. She was sure of the Heidens, but she had to put the feelings into words. "They know what it is to be hated without no reason. Mr. Heiden was born in Germany, and some folks around here don't take to that. Besides, they're my friends."

"I've got things"—he used his head to point—"in a cave back that way. I was trying to make it from there to water when I passed out." He hesitated, his voice changing. "I hate to ask more of you."

She was getting up. "I'll get your gear. Is the cave easy to spot?"

He raised himself up on one elbow. "About twenty-five or thirty feet. Look to your left where the hill goes up behind a stand of cedars. You'll see my path. I've used it lots to get out of the rain."

She moved away. Then, stopping, she looked back, reluctant to leave him. "Rest. You just rest." When the trees blocked her view of him, her pace quickened. Hurry, she told herself.

In the dim cave Hallie found his belongings. She touched the small stack of books and looked quickly through a pad of drawings. From one picture the startled eyes of a bobcat stared up at her. "Lands." She was shaking her head. "It don't seem possible a person could draw like that." Then remembering the time, she placed the books, pad, and some art utensils into a burlap bag that contained a few articles of clothing. On a nearby rock was a kettle and a skillet, but Hallie left them. No use to tote things like that.

Then she was ready to step back out into the sunlight. She stood listening to the sound of rustling leaves, and fear possessed her once more. They could be there on the other side of the bush. Elton and Roscoe could be there, and she had left her knife by the water.

With her hands clenched and her breath held, she stepped from behind the trees. There was no sound except the call of a crow from a nearby tree.

"I'm coming, Johnny. Oh, I'm coming," she called when

she saw him. He was asleep again, but this time she did not fear that he was dead. She touched his shoulder. "We've got to go now."

"Hallie," he said. "There aren't any words to thank you."

Her eyes looked into his blue ones. "Reckon we don't need words. You saved me. Now I'm helping you." But it was more than that, she knew. In the beginning she had come because of obligation. Now she did what she did, would do whatever was necessary, not because of obligation, but for him, for Johnny Childers. It was time to move.

With Beauty tied just below the large flat rock where he rested, getting the man onto the horse's back was not as big a task as she had feared. "Things is working out real good," she announced as she tied him to the saddle with the rope she was proud of having brought. "Now you don't have to be afeard of falling off. Just rest yourself." The move had exhausted him, and his eyes closed. "Helga will make you soup," Hallie promised.

Her thoughts were not as optimistic as her words. If anyone came now, there would be no hiding. Beauty's hoofs on the mountainside seemed deafeningly loud. Johnny's bag was tied securely to the horse, but Hallie clutched the flour sack, empty now except for the poultice medicine and the knife, tightly under her arm. Somewhere above her, a mountain cat cried. Once cougars had been creatures Hallie feared. Now the hills held no terrors except man. It was her own kind that made Hallie dread each forward step.

Unmindful of her fears, Childers rested against Beauty's

neck. When the pain became too much for him, he would groan softly, and Hallie would bite her lip in sympathy.

When they were at last in the dark barn, she touched his shoulder. "We got to get you in the wagon now and hid. There could be folks on the trail from here out."

Standing in the wagon she lifted his legs over the edge and slid him from the horse, easing his fall with her body.

Her plan had been laid earlier. She knew what to do. When the horses were hitched, she ran to the stalks cut from the summer's cornfield. They stood stacked upright like pyramids waiting to be fodder for the stock's winter meals. Yes, they would do. Hurry, hurry. Pa could come into the barn at any time. Her mind raced, but there was no story to explain why she was stacking the corn stalks in the wagon. Pa would walk over to look in, and he would see Johnny Childers. Then what? What would Pa do? There was no tellin', no way to guess. It just must not happen. She had to be well down the road before Pa came back to the cabin.

"I've got you covered now real good," she told Childers. "I'll just leave space for you to breathe and see. Then if anyone comes toward us, I'll lean back, cover your face real quick, and let on like I just wanted to pick up this basket. You ready?"

"Yes."

"We can't go too fast on the trail, but still it'll be a bumpy ride." When they were out of the yard, she breathed easy for the first time.

For a while the trail was clear. Hallie began to feel less

worried, and her hand relaxed a little on the reins. "You okay?" she called, but there was no answer from the wagon bed. "Just sleep," she said. "You just sleep."

Suddenly there was a movement in the trees near the edge of the road. The flour sack with the knife was on the seat beside her, and she reached to pull it into her lap when she recognized the men. "Oh, God, it's them," she whispered.

Elton and Roscoe were by the road. There was no time to reach back for the basket. "Giddy up," she called out to the horses. She saw Elton hold up his hand, but then she fastened her eyes to the road ahead. She wouldn't stop even if they stepped in front of her. She wouldn't stop even if they fired their guns.

The dust from the trail swirled through the air. "Fool, girl," yelled one of the men, but Hallie did not look back.

The wagon bounced down the road. "Hold on," Hallie called. "We got to move fast now." When they had gone far enough, she let the horses slow and then stop. Turning on the seat, she reached back and brushed a corn stalk from Childers's face. His eyes were closed. "He's not dead," she said. "God, you wouldn't take him away from me now, would you? He's asleep. He's sleepy from sickness and maybe from the medicine, but he ain't dead." She urged Red and Doc on by calling, "Get up. We got to get to help quick."

At the turn, Hallie had to slow down. It wasn't far now. First she had to pass Harp Otis's little house. Hallie waved to Harp, who was in front of his cabin building a fire under a big black kettle. She would tell Johnny about Dewey riding

Harp's horse. It was a story that would make Johnny smile. There would be time for sharing stories. There had to be.

In front of the Heidens' neat white house, Hallie stopped the horses. Twisting on the seat, she began to throw the stalks away from Johnny until her hand was on his chest and feeling his breaths. "Wait right here," she said. "You just wait right here."

She jumped from the seat. The dogs were barking, and Hallie saw Helga come out onto the porch. Kurt Heiden was coming toward her from the barn. Suddenly Hallie felt as if her legs might give way. She leaned heavily on the gate post, and the haystack near the fence seemed to move up and down before her eyes.

"Something's wrong," Helga called.

"I'll come carry you," shouted Mr. Heiden, breaking into a run.

"No, please," Hallie pulled herself up straight. "You got to lift Johnny. You got to help my friend Johnny."

10

INSTALLED IN THE HEIDENS' SPARE ROOM with a poultice on his leg and stew in his stomach, Johnny was better even before Hallie had to leave for home.

"*Ja*, the leg it must be up," Kurt Heiden had insisted. "No journey for you, not for a time."

Hallie turned quickly away, amazed and startled by her gladness. Johnny Childers would not go away from her, not today. When he fell asleep, she lingered at the foot of his bed until Helga came to the bedroom door.

"I'm leaving," Hallie whispered, but she did not meet her friend's eyes until they were outside on the brick walk. "He'll be a burden to you," she said then.

"There's Kurin to help. Maybe doing for Mr. Childers might take her mind off being kept out of school."

"Still . . ." Hallie reached for the gate, but she did not push at it. "Still, I think I'll come. It's my duty to see to him."

"Your duty?"

Hallie felt Helga looking at her. She also felt the heat rising to her face. "It's not what you think." She swallowed hard. "I'm not fool enough to go sweet on Johnny Childers. I'm beholden. That's all. I never told you about Gid Jones."

She gripped the gate hard enough to make her knuckles white.

Helga covered Hallie's hand with her own. "What, Hallie? What about Gid?"

"Except for Johnny saving me, no telling what would of happened to me. That's all."

"When? What happened?"

"Gid jumped me on the trail." Hallie pushed against the gate and spoke over the creaking. "No need talking about it now, but I'm obligated to Johnny Childers, real obligated." She hurried to the wagon.

Helga followed. "He's handsome, though," she said when Hallie was settled on the seat. "You'll get to know each other pretty well, I guess."

Hallie, pretending not to hear, called, "Get up," much louder than was necessary.

Her mind rolled faster than the wheels. She had to go each day to Heidens', had to be there until Johnny was ready to ride away. She had saved him, and now for just a time he was hers to care for, but what could she tell Pa?

No answer had come to her by the time she reached home, and she groaned when she saw Mason near the barn. He looked up from the rail fence he worked on. "Where you been?" he called.

"Heidens'."

He came to lift the wooden harness hames, freeing the horses. "Don't know as you ought to be spending a lot of

time there. Feeling in town's running right strong against Kurt Heiden."

"What could happen to me just visiting?" She turned her back and walked a few steps before adding to the lie. "Besides, Helga's sick and needs cheering."

"Well, then, you'll have to ride Beauty." There was no argument in his voice. "Fellow up here today from the sawmill, said I could have a few weeks' work. Reckon I might as well carry the younguns to school as I go."

She swung to face him, clapping her hands. "Wonderful! Ain't it wonderful!"

"We can use the cash money, that's for sure." He looked at her closely, but the girl ignored him, hurrying away toward the cabin.

Waking the next morning, Hallie faced the first truly happy day since her mother's death. She would change the poultice on Johnny's leg, wash his face and hands with a cloth, carry his food. "Rise and shine," she called to the young ones. "It's just bound to be a beautiful day."

Amid the packing of the lunch buckets, she stopped suddenly, the knife halfway through a loaf of bread. "Don't go being no blamed fool," she cautioned herself, but still her mind rushed to decide which chores had to be done, which could be postponed. And just before running to the barn, she arranged her hair up on top of her head.

"Beauty," she said, stroking his sleek side before she cinched the saddle, "can't nothing get me down today." She

sang as she rode, and her song bounced against the trees and rocks.

Mary, however, had news that did threaten to get Hallie down and made her wish the visit with Pearly had been assigned to the list of put-off chores.

Quiet when she opened the door, the woman held off at first. Then she settled her bulk into a chair next to the one where Hallie rocked Pearly. "Something needs saying." She leaned over to the rocker arm and slowed Hallie's movement. "Gid's back."

Hallie jumbed to her feet, but Mary reached out to clutch the girl's skirt and pull her down into the chair. "Wait now and hear me out. He showed up last night. Hurt. All red and scarred from German gas. Can't see out of but one eye."

"Gid's done been in the fighting?" Hallie was surprised. Star's last letter spoke of leaving soon for France. She wouldn't have thought Gid to be that far ahead of him.

"I had to take him in. Pitiful thing. Break any heart to look at him."

Hallie studied the well-scrubbed floor and doubted her ability to feel sympathy for Gid Jones, scarred or not. "I won't come here no more," she said softly.

"No, now, child." Mary put a big hand on Hallie's arm. "You got nothing to fear. Iffen I didn't know it as a sure fact, he wouldn't be here. Ain't no strength left in Gid for trouble." She shook her head. "You won't have to fret none about Gid."

Hallie's mind rushed. She couldn't take Pearly now. In a few days Johnny would be gone. "I'll be taking the baby soon. Then you can come visit me at my place." She gave Mary a brave smile.

"I knew you'd see the way of it. Had to take him in. Hurt like he is."

Hallie looked out the window. "He won't follow after me when I go?"

"My word, he won't."

Hallie wasn't convinced, but then she brightened. "I'm on Beauty. Gid couldn't stop me anyways."

And when she was up on the horse and moving down the autumn trail, it took only a minute to dismiss Gid Jones. Got what he deserved, Hallie thought. His injury troubled her only in that it made the war more real. Star would be fighting soon. It would be possible then for Star to be injured or even killed. She shivered. Thank the Lord Johnny didn't believe in this war.

Knowing she shouldn't, she let her mind fill with his face. She had never known a man like Johnny Childers, and the feelings he stirred in her were unfamiliar ones too.

Thinking about Johnny was easier than facing him, stronger, smiling, and ready to talk. Hallie could not meet his clear blue eyes. She moved slowly to the edge of his bed and kept her gaze on the diamond design of the quilt.

With the sick Johnny, she had felt confident. Now when finally she looked at his face, she saw his education and his knowledge of the world beyond the hills.

"Hallie." He held out his hand to her, and timidly she took it. "I've been thinking and thinking about you."

She searched for words but was aware only of the redness of her face and the roughness of the hand Johnny held. She pulled away. "You're perkier," she muttered.

"You don't seem very pleased. Maybe you liked me better when I was dying." He laughed.

"No, I . . ." She shrugged her shoulders. "Reckon I ain't accustomed to talking much to city folks."

"Now, Hallie," he admonished, "bet I know the hills around your place as well as you do. Had you ever seen that little cave before? And you know what, I can tell you where there's a litter of newborn bobcats. Besides, I thought we were friends." He looked sad.

Funning me, she thought, but still, she could not chance it, could not bear to be the cause of his sadness. "We are," she said. "I'm just a tongue-tied mountain boomer."

"No." He shifted in the bed and leaned nearer to her. "You, Hallie, are a brave woman, as brave as Clara Barton. Do you know who she was?"

"Yes." He figures I'm stupid, she thought, and she considered telling him about her score on her eighth-grade exam, but he began to talk again.

"Would you like to go to school? Maybe be a nurse like Clara Barton?"

"No." Her eyes sought the window and held to the haystack outside it. "No, I used to think some about how it'd be to be a teacher."

"Fine! A teacher would be fine. You, Hallie, are a brave woman, a woman who deserves to find her place in the world."

Woman. She studied the hay and the pitchfork stuck in it. He was calling her a woman, not a girl, but her delight was mixed with anger. Johnny Childers had no right to dig at sore spots, old dreams long ago given up.

"There ain't no way." The flatness of her tone dismissed the idea.

"But there is a way." The excitement in his voice made her look at him. He was smiling. "Hallie, my aunt lives in Tahlequah. You could stay with her and go to normal school. Aunt Abby'd like having you. She'd want to help the girl who saved my life."

"You don't owe me." She pressed her lips together hard.

"Let me do it then because we're friends."

"There's the young ones and the baby." Her heart raced. "Couldn't leave them."

"Think it over. Normal school doesn't take so long. Consider what you could do for them later, when you're finished."

Don't get all het up, Hallie warned herself, but it did no good. She looked at the door. Maybe she should run out of the room and back up into the hills, but she knew she wouldn't. In one hand was the newspaper she'd carried with her from the kitchen.

"You want to see the Stigler paper?" She pushed it

toward him. "Heidens' hired hand brought the mail, and the paper comes in it."

"A teacher, sure. You'll be a good teacher." He nodded his head as if agreeing to a plan. Then he lay back and closed his eyes. "I'd like to have you read to me."

She pulled a chair next to the bed and spread the paper open over the bright cover.

" 'The tide may have turned in Europe, but fledgling American doughboys keep pouring into training camps in unpredicted numbers. Thus far, about three million men have been drafted, with some one million volunteers and their steady arrival in Europe is celebrated.' "

Suddenly she stopped reading. His eyes were open, his face twisted, and his hands were clenched into fists. "I'm sorry," she murmured. "Should of knowed not to read that."

He shrugged. "I can't hide from the damn war. Can't hide from the news." He tried to smile. "The war's everywhere. I'll go to jail. Got to accept it." Misery dripped from his voice. "I thought I'd come to terms." He took a deep breath. "But I had plans, Hallie. I had plans before this blasted war came along."

She jumped to her feet. "You can go back to the hills. When your leg's healed some, you can go back up. I'll bring you food, Johnny. Promise I will."

"No. No more hiding." He closed his eyes again. "Read something. Something else."

She eased back into the chair. For a moment she studied

his face. He was older than Star, had to be to be drafted, but suddenly she thought he looked younger, like Brack. She wanted to make him forget the war. She reached for the paper and began. " 'Wearing yellow and purple ribbons across their chests, ladies from Stigler were joined by their sisters from surrounding areas for a parade encouraging the vote for women.' Look." She held the picture for Johnny to see.

He pushed up on his elbow. "Wouldn't surprise me to see my aunt in that picture. She's working to get women the vote."

Hallie leaned closer. "My mercy!" she shouted, pointing. "There's Mrs. Atkins, and she's got on her patent leather shoes. Just think, a woman from Lafine marching for the vote." Forgetting her shyness, Hallie told Johnny all about Miss Clark's dismissal and about Mrs. Atkins's shoes.

Johnny lay back on his pillow while she talked. Suddenly she stopped. "I'm rattling on." She stood and moved away from the bed.

"No. Come back. Please. I love your stories. So will your students."

His smile drew her back to his bedside, and she picked up the paper. "They're having real moving pictures at the Lyric Theater." She held up the advertisement, reading to him, *"His Fatal Beauty*, a one-reel comedy."

"Have you ever been to a picture show?" he asked.

"No, but tent shows come to Lafine. We went once."

"I wish I could take you. Maybe see Charlie Chaplin. He

always makes me laugh. I'd love to drive my car up to your door and take you to a picture show. You'd go, wouldn't you, Hallie?"

She nodded. Then she laughed. "I don't know as a car could get to my door, though."

"I'll get a horse," he said, and he closed his eyes. "We'll go to a woman's suffrage rally too. You'd like to vote, right, Hallie? You're a modern woman."

"That'd be nice," she murmured, and she wanted to close her eyes too, longed to join his dreaming.

"Who knows? When everything is faced and settled." A sad note slipped into his voice, and Hallie bit at her fingernail, but the sorrow was gone when he went on. "And we might find a fair where we can ride a Ferris wheel." He smiled. "That's something I've been wanting to do. Bet up there above everything the world's troubles would seem smaller."

A picture came to Hallie's mind, one she had seen on Mrs. Atkins's stereoscope, of the Columbian Exposition. A smartly dressed lady and gentleman stood in front of a Ferris wheel. For an instant she was the lady with Johnny beside her. "A modern woman and her beau," she imagined might be printed beneath the picture.

Then she gave herself a little shake. "Don't go getting carried away," she knew Ma would have said.

But Johnny's smile made her forget the warning. "Would you be afraid way up on a Ferris wheel?" he asked.

"Scared plumb to death, but at least I'd die happy."

Even on the trip home Hallie kept imagining herself with

Johnny at a picture show or on a Ferris wheel. During supper the young ones chattered as usual, but her thoughts traced Johnny's words. Later, going out to check on Dovie and Burch, who were gathering kindling wood, she forgot the children and stood gazing at the pink of the sunset, drifting through the trees. "A modern woman," she said aloud.

"What's a modern woman?" Dovie's voice interrupted.

Hallie sat down on a stump and pulled her little sister to her. "Why, a modern woman is a lady who finds her place in the world. She fights for the vote, and she does the work she wants to do. Dovie, did you know some ladies even work in factories and make air machines? I read about them in the *Stigler Sentinel.*"

"Are you a lady now or just a girl?" Dovie leaned out to study Hallie's face.

"Reckon I'm a lady now." Hallie's confidence grew as she spoke. "I'm a brave modern woman ready to find my place in the world. You and Burch take the kindling on in. I'll come along in a spell." What if she could go to normal school? Oh, what if she really could? It was too powerful even to think about. Hallie stared at the pink glow and thought only that it seemed especially beautiful. Then she bent, picked up one more piece of kindling, and headed back into the cabin.

ON THE AFTERNOON OF THE FOURTH MORNING, Hallie stopped in the middle of making her X on the calendar, marking the days until Star's return. "You're marking off other days too," she whispered to herself, and her pencil felt heavy in her hand. Johnny was stronger. He would not tarry long in the Heidens' spare room. She hurried through the breakfast cleanup she had postponed in the morning.

"She was. He was. It was. They were," she recited, and she poured the heated water over the bowls.

"Get these down and you'll be ready for normal school," he had said when he handed her the list of verbs.

She had not responded, could never respond to his mention of going on to school. Nor could she bear to think of his leaving. "She doesn't. He doesn't. It doesn't. They don't." Without really seeing it, she wiped at the dried mush on a bowl. "They don't. They don't have much more time." If he goes away, and you stay here. You ain't, aren't likely to ever see him again, she thought.

By the time she began to make biscuits for supper, Hallie had almost made up her mind to talk to Johnny about his normal school offer. Rolling out the dough, she tried to imagine the family without her, but she couldn't. Dovie and Burch had school to keep them busy, but who would cook supper? And of course there was little Pearly. Next week he too would be living in the cabin.

Hallie was dipping up gravy when the boys and Mason came in from chores, bringing Ruby with them. "I didn't want to come at suppertime," the visitor explained, "but lands, I been over here a slew of times lately. There ain't never anybody to home daytimes."

Hallie shook her head quickly at Ruby, holding her hands

to her lips. Mason and the boys were washing up. They had not noticed. "I ain't hungry," she said to Ruby. "We can talk in the other room. Here, Turner, you can finish taking up the food."

"Hallie Horton," Ruby accused when they were safely settled on the edge of Hallie's bed. "You got secrets."

"No, I just don't want Pa to know how much time I been spending over to Heidens'. That's all. He claims I ain't safe there, folks thinking like they do."

"Might be he's right. I've heard lots of talk about how all Germans ought to be run out of the country." Hallie wanted to protest, but Ruby, bursting with news, did not give her a chance. "I do got a secret."

"Tell it then."

Ruby squealed with happiness. "Me and Erwart is fixing to run off and get married." She held up her three fingers to indicate the days. "Come Saturday, I'll be Mrs. Erwart Tanner Junior."

Hallie hugged her friend. "I'm glad. Real glad for you, Ruby."

"His ma's going to have a sure enough hissy." Ruby did not seem really troubled. She bounced on Hallie's bed. But then her face was serious. "I do hope you'll find you a man, Hallie. Love is plumb wonderful, just like the songs say."

Hallie smiled. "I expect it is, Ruby. I just expect you're right about that. Where will you live after you're married?"

"Ain't this a hoot? Going to live right in the rooming house. I'll be one of Mrs. Bailey's precious roomers."

"Vida Mae? Will she still be working for Mrs. Bailey?"

"Lands no, girl. That's why I'm back home. Mrs. Bailey let us both go on account of the high line moving. Ma says Vida Mae's got to find a job or marry number fifteen as soon as he's free."

"If she made just a little bit"—Hallie tried to keep her voice casual—"say for helping out a family. Do you reckon that would be enough?"

"Vida Mae is awful desperate. You know about some job?"

"No." Hallie jumped up to walk around the room. "I was just trying to think. It'd be a shame to see Vida Mae have to marry number fifteen."

Later that evening Mason sat on the porch smoking his pipe. Drawing herself up straight for strength, Hallie slipped out the door to stand beside him. "If I could find a way, would you bar me from going to normal school over to Tahlequah?" She blurted out the words before losing courage.

"There ain't no money, daughter. You know that?"

"But was I to find a way?"

He took out his pipe and turned to look at her. "There's the baby. What could we do with him?"

"If I worked it all out?"

"That be a powerful lot of working out." He shrugged his shoulders. "If some miracle was to come, I'd not oppose you." He wiped at his face. "Lost one youngun that way, and now he's about to be shot at. Besides, this family's mine, not yours. Reckon it's time I took more of a hand in their raising."

He stood and walked quickly into the trees. Hallie breathed deeply and sank into his vacant chair.

That night sleep did not come easily. In her narrow bed she lay planning. Tomorrow, after seeing Pearly, she would go to Johnny. She would tell him she wanted to go to normal school. Finally she slipped into dreams of their next meeting.

In the morning everything seemed to go wrong. The biscuits almost burned. Turner spilled half the contents of the milk bucket he brought in from the barn, and Dovie cried because Burch called her squirt. "A person might rather be married to number fifteen than take on this bunch," Hallie muttered to herself in the kitchen, but nothing could really get her down. Johnny was waiting for her.

She ran to the mirror over the washstand to appraise the reflection, moving away quickly when her father came in to wash.

When they were gone, her hands flew over preparations for leaving. Quickly she washed the breakfast dishes. Clothes needed doing up, but they could wait. Tomorrow she could do more chores.

At the cutoff to the Jones place she considered skipping the visit with Pearly, but she turned the horse in that direction. "Time will come when I ain't here to see him," she said aloud. Could she really leave the hills? She stopped the horse for just a minute and sat listening to the voice of the creek as it moved over the rocks and vibrated through the trees.

Mary was at the door waiting. "I'm right glad to see you. You all right?" She leaned toward Hallie, studying the girl's face.

It took Hallie only a second to understand the concern. "I'm fine. Mary, where's Gid at?"

"Don't get all in an uproar, now." The woman put out a big hand and guided Hallie to a chair. "Me and Gid we had a row on account of news brung me by an army fellow. I never said he had to go, but he went storming out of here. Likely spent the night up by the still, drinking. I expect when he comes to, he'll come slinking back, begging me to let him stay." She shrugged her shoulders. "I got to study on what to do about Gid."

Hallie couldn't be bothered about Gid Jones or even with Mary's indecision. Tomorrow she would ask what the army man had said. Gid Jones was like dirty clothes. He could be put off for a day. For now she wanted only to kiss Pearly and to be out on Beauty riding toward Johnny. Gid Jones did not matter now. Nothing could touch her now.

Out on the trail again, she let Beauty trot. It was November. Most of the trees were bare, but the sun shone warmly on the empty limbs. The pine trees seemed more splendid among their leafless neighbors. "It's a beautiful day for a ride," Hallie said. "A beautiful day to spend with Johnny."

But when she walked into Johnny's room, Hallie was

shocked to find him standing up. "I'm stronger," he told her. "Strong enough to go."

Fighting the protest that rose in her throat, she sank into a chair. He paced, limping from the window to the bed and back to the window.

He's nervous, she thought, all nervous about what's ahead for him. She would make him feel better. "There might be a way. You know, what you said about normal school."

He came back then to sit on the bed, and while she told him about Vida Mae, he smiled. "I'd have to earn enough to pay her wage."

"Wonderful. It's a deal." He took her hand and held it. "We'll find you a job. Aunt Abby will help. We'll make sure you can pay Vida Mae."

Hallie was conscious of her hand in his, too conscious to think clearly, but she made no attempt to pull away.

"You've got good times ahead, Hallie." She felt the pressure of his fingers increase on hers. "And maybe if my trouble doesn't last too long, you'll let me be part of them."

She wanted to declare that she would wait, wait forever if necessary, but she knew it was too soon to be talking so. "I brought up school to my pa," she said.

"Want me to talk to him?"

"No." She shook her head. "I'll do it. She laughed. "I'll just threaten to join up with the army."

He released her hand and stretched out on the bed, his arms behind his head. "You could go right away. Start to work and settle in before the term starts after Christmas."

A sudden loneliness came to her. "But for Christmas I'd have to be home. I'd not be away from the young ones at Christmas."

He nodded his understanding. "Home on the train and bringing presents. How would that strike you?"

Hallie closed her eyes. "Makes me quiver just picturing it."

11

IT WAS A STRANGE DAY. Johnny did not speak at all of how he would leave. Hallie wandered out to the barn to hear the plan from Mr. Heiden. Luke, the hired man who had been given the day off, would come back just after dark to drive to Stigler. Johnny would be his passenger. Luke would return the next evening with supplies, but the passenger would be gone, gone on the train to face a trial.

Johnny's mood changed frequently. He passed a good part of the morning reciting limericks for Hallie and Kurin. He ended by taking up his art pen and pencil. "There was a young man of Bengal, who went to a fancy-dress ball. He went just for fun, dressed up as a bun, and a dog ate him up in the hall," he recited, and as he talked he drew, giving the illustration to the delighted Kurin. Then he put down the pad, grew very quiet, and went outside alone. Hallie watched as he limped to the big pine in the side yard. When he rested his head on the forearm he had leaned against the tree, Hallie turned away from the window.

During the noon meal he told jokes, and Hallie, trying to be part of the lightness, told the story about Watch and the buttermilk.

"Now that deserves a poem," said Johnny. "And I shall have composed a masterpiece before I finish this pie."

For a few minutes they ate in silence, and Johnny gave Kurin a look of mock reproach when she giggled. "I have it," he announced when the last bit of apple pie had been chewed. "There once was a dog from Lafine, who on Hallie's buttermilk did dine. He wagged his tail twice, and said, 'Now that's nice, But it's really for chicken I pine.' "

The others laughed, and Hallie tried to smile, but the grandfather clock in the parlor was striking one.

"I'd like to be here when he goes," Hallie told Helga as she stacked dishes on the sideboard.

"You're always welcome to stay the night." Helga looked up from taking up the leftover dumplings and smiled. "He's a good man. I'm glad for you, my friend."

"Too soon to be saying such," Hallie protested, but she sang as she rode into town to tell the young ones not to expect her home. She found them at recess. The boys, who had been playing marbles, complained about the interruption and went quickly back to their game. Dovie, however, lingered. "I wanted to practice my numbers for you," she said, and pulled at Hallie's hand.

The older girl stared down at the little one. How can I ever go off to normal and leave her? she questioned herself. "I'll bring you a stick of licorice tomorrow. I've got some pennies, and I'll go by the store on my way home." She bent down to hug Dovie. "I'll see to what you need all your time in school, Dovie. If I get more schooling, I can buy you dresses and pretty ribbons."

Dovie's face twisted in confusion. "But you already finished, done took the exam and everything."

"Never you mind. Just run back and play. Tell Pa I'm staying at Helga's. The licorice will be waiting for you tomorrow." Hallie did not look back at the school as she rode away.

Elton Holmes and Roscoe Williams were tying their horses in front of the store when Hallie came out from having stopped for the mail. Clutching Star's letter close, she kept her eyes on the ground and hurried to her horse. From atop Beauty, she watched their backs as they disappeared into the building, and a shiver went over her body. "Thank the Lord they never had a chance to get at Johnny," she whispered to the horse, and she pressed his sides with her knees to urge him on.

Johnny and Helga were both sitting in the parlor when Hallie got back to the house. Helga's eyes lit up. "Is that a letter from Star?"

"Yes."

"Would you read it to us? I haven't had one this week."

Hallie glanced at Johnny. "I've read it. Stopped on the way. Johnny wouldn't be interested."

"I would if you want to share it." He motioned for her to sit beside him on the settee. "Your brother's at war. It's right for him, and I'm concerned with you about his safety."

It was a short letter. "Dear Hallie," she read. "It seems like a terrible long time since I left home. Reckon it's starting to get cool there and the trees are turning. I wonder will I ever walk those old home trails again. Tomorrow we leave for France. Some of the boys can't wait to get into the fray. Oh, Hallie, you never seen such a bunch for swaggering and threatening the Huns. Guess it gets their courage up, but I don't mind saying it wouldn't dissatisfy me none if it was over before I got there. I aim to do my duty, but the thought of pointing my gun at another man 'stead of a rabbit ain't one I'm hankering after. Tell Pa and the kids I say hello. I'll write more later. Your brother, Star."

Tears streamed down Hallie's cheeks as she read. When Helga, who was crying too, slipped silently from the room, Johnny slid over to Hallie and put his arms gently across her shoulders.

"My brother's special," she told him. "He's obliged to stay safe. I lost my ma," she said simply, as if she had never realized the fact before. "My ma died, and my brother might die too." Her silent tears became sobs now, and she leaned against him.

"Just cry, Hallie," he whispered, and he stroked her hair.

"I never do," she murmured, "not to be seen."

"It's all right. You don't always have to be strong."

They sat silently together, and for a time as Hallie cried freely she felt a peace she had not known since her mother's death. But then she noticed the slant of the sun through the lace curtains. "Oh," she wiped at her eyes. "It's getting late."

Johnny stood and limped to the window. "We've got to

believe my trouble will pass." He turned back to smile at her. "We'll think about riding a Ferris wheel."

While Helga and Kurin were busy in the kitchen, Hallie and Johnny sat in the porch swing. The sun was beginning to set, and Hallie felt as if the pink glow were inside her. "I'll remember this always," she told Johnny when he took her hand.

He smiled. "There will be so many more times together, Hallie. That's what we've got to hold to, that we will have other sunsets to watch."

They stayed in the swing until called for supper. It was a glorious meal with ham and sweet potatoes and great yeast rolls. "You worked too hard," Johnny said, but his appetite pleased Helga.

When they had finished the peach cobbler, Helga stood and went toward the parlor. "Hallie," she called over her shoulder, "you and Johnny come in here while I clear the table. You don't have long. I'll just wind the Victrola."

Hallie felt shy and studied her empty plate, but Johnny laughed, took her hand, and led the way. "We could try dancing a little," he said, "if you don't mind a gimp leg."

In his arms, she forgot all embarrassment, and felt as if she belonged there. Beginning to move slowly, they were so lost in the music and in each other that even the gunshot did not, at once, disturb them. It was Helga's scream and Kurt's thundering, "What? What has happened?" that made them stop turning.

"The hay barn," Kurin screamed. "There's fire in the hay barn."

"My gun!" Kurt's running feet vibrated through the house.

Johnny bolted toward the kitchen with Hallie behind him. "Wait. Let me go with you."

Hallie saw Kurt reach for another gun and hand it to Johnny, but everything seemed to be happening with exaggerated slowness. This was the trouble her father had feared. Everyone, it appeared to her, was moving through deep water. She wanted to reach out to stop Johnny, but her arms felt too heavy to move.

"Papa," Helga pleaded. "Don't go. Please."

"I have to, daughter. Next might be the house." He was out the door, and Johnny was behind him. With one great burst Hallie was beside him.

"No," she begged. Johnny's hand was on the doorknob, but she grabbed his arm.

"Have to, Hallie. There's a time to fight." He moved away from her and was gone out the door.

Still feeling as if she were in a dream, Hallie watched. "They'll be killed," she said without emotion. Whoever was there, she reasoned, had fired the shot, had fired it to bring attention to the barn. The were waiting, waiting in the dark.

"They can't kill my papa." Kurin moved toward a window.

Helga grabbed her sister's skirts and pulled her back.

"Stay away from the window," she said. "There's nothing we can do."

Suddenly Hallie was awake. "We'll fight," she contradicted, reaching for the butcher knife. "I'll cut out the heart of ary a man comes in that door."

Outside there was no noise. For a quiet second the older girls looked at each other. "Yes," said Helga, "we'll fight." She took up the iron skillet.

The memory of the day Turner rode Harp's horse came to Hallie. Turning to the sobbing Kurin, she put her hands on the little girl's shoulders. "Go get under the bed. Get under the bed and don't come out for anything. Unless the house is on fire, you just stay right still under that bed."

When Kurin was out of the room, the girls, with their weapons above their heads, stationed themselves behind the outside door. All was quiet, and they stood listening. Helga smiled bravely. Then there was a sound from the living room, the rocking chair moving against the hard floor. Something had bumped it.

We're behind the wrong door, Hallie thought, but it was too late.

"Howdy, ladies." It was a horrible voice, one Hallie hated. Gid Jones stood before her. "I done come in front like company." A rifle was in his hand, and he aimed it at Hallie.

Helga screamed and dropped the skillet. "My papa? What did you do to my papa?"

"Oh, he can't come back in. Might say he got tied up

outside." Gid laughed. "Got tied up, that's a joke." He poked the gun toward the girls. "Why ain't you laughing?"

Hallie's eyes were darting around the room. Sweat ran down her face. What could she do? The knife was still in her hand, but there was no way to hurt Gid. I would if I could, she thought. It wouldn't fret me none to use it on him.

She looked at him. His face and neck were terrible, great red welts of scars, one eye almost closed. Wondering about the battle that had resulted in such horrible injury, Hallie forgot for a fleeting second about the gun, but then Gid jabbed the steel barrel into Helga's ribs. His words, though, were for Hallie. "Iffen you don't want me to blow up Fraulein here, you best be dropping that there knife."

The knife fell from Hallie's fingers and clattered against the floor. "Now." Gid motioned with his head. "You two just walk real easy like over to the table and set yourself down. Iffen you're real good, reckon we might let you watch the hanging."

"Gid, please." Hallie was frantic, her body shaking. "I'll do anything." Disgusting images flashed through her mind, but she went on, "anything you want me to. Just don't hurt no one. There ain't anyone here ever done any harm."

Gid spat on the floor. "The law don't see it that way. The law says it's a sure enough crime not to fight for your country." He moved his gun to jab at Helga. "We weren't aiming to kill the German, just rough him up some. But now we know he's been hiding that yellow-belly coward." He smiled. "You know, it's damn lucky I come along. Them other boys, they wouldn't of knowed the slacker like I done." He snarled at Hallie. "I seen him real good the day he stuck his nose into what weren't none of his business."

It's my fault. The knowledge came full blown to Hallie. Gid knew Johnny because of that day by the creek. I brought Johnny here for Mr. Heiden to take in. They are both going to die because of me. She clenched her fists. It couldn't happen. She had to stop it. Somehow, she had to stop what was happening outside in the dark.

There were steps on the back porch. Elton and Roscoe erupted, cursing, through the door. "Hey," Elton reached out to touch one of Helga's braids, "You got women, Gid. Now you got to share."

Gid shrugged his shoulders. "You can have the fraulein, but that one"—he pointed his gun at Hallie—"I got me a score to settle with that one there soon as we're done with the hangings."

Hallie stared into the disfigured face. Do what you please with me, she thought. What could it matter? If they killed Johnny, what could anything they would do to her matter?

"You know," Roscoe's voice sounded nervous. "I been doing me some studying on hanging them two fellows."

"You losing your nerve, Williams?" Elton grunted.

He gestured emphatically with his hands. "Not losing my nerve. Just using my head, maybe. Why not take them two fellows into town for hanging? We might get into some real hot water do we just string them up our ownselves."

"I ain't wanting to wait around for no trial." Gid was

shaking his head. "I'm aiming to get out of these here parts. I want to see that yellow belly hang 'fore I go."

Roscoe didn't give up. "Dad could be roused up. Have the trial tonight and the hanging. You talk to Dad, Gid, all injured in the war and everything. He'll listen to you sure."

"Might be the best idea, all right." Elton was stroking his hairy chin, considering. He turned to Gid. "Naturally, it don't matter to you none, leaving like you are. Me and Roscoe, though, we got to stay right here. Might not hurt none to have the law's sayso on our side. That hired fellow didn't like it none, us running him off. Folks like that could cause us trouble."

Hope exploded in Hallie's brain. There would be time. Time to save Johnny and Mr. Heiden. The grandfather clock struck seven. There would be time, but it would be up to her. Half hidden by the potato basket, the knife still lay on the floor beside the wall.

"Well, then." Gid was clearly disappointed. "Iffen you're bound and determined to take 'em back to town, let's get them fellows loaded up in the wagon."

"These two? What about them? Roscoe asked.

"You and Elton both got rope left, hanging on your arms plain as the nose on your face. Can't you handle tying up two helpless women?" Gid spat with disguist.

Maybe they will fight, Hallie thought. If they would only fight, I might be able to reach the knife. But nothing more was said, and Gid stomped toward the door.

"Get your hands behind your back and your feet together." Elton began to tie Hallie while Roscoe worked on Helga.

Standing in the doorway, Gid turned back. "Do what you want with the other one, but I'm taking that Horton thing with me. Fixing to have me a little fun, I am." He leered at Hallie, and she turned her face away. "Hurry up, you two. I'll get the wagon ready."

"Who died and left him king?" Roscoe muttered to Elton when Gid was gone. "We was looking for that slacker our ownselves long before he mixed in."

"Don't get riled." Elton quickly wrapped Hallie's feet. "We need Gid standing up for folks to see. Going to make a real stir. Gid's a sure-enough hero while that there Childers been hiding in the bushes."

Roscoe gave a hard jerk on the rope he wrapped around Helga's ankles. "There now, you ladies rest yourselves real easy." And they were gone out the door.

"Kurin." Hallie's voice was low but strong. "Kurin, quick run here." There was no movement from the room next door.

Helga shook her head. "No, they might come back."

"Just for the knife." Hallie's voice became pleading. "Please Kurin, just quick for the knife. Crawl. Stay on the floor."

There was a rustle. On hands and knees, the little girl, blond braids swinging, moved quickly into the room. "By the tater basket." Hallie motioned with her head. "Crawl, quick." Hallie kept her eyes on the door, praying. If they came back, if they came back and hurt Kurin, that too would be her fault.

Kurin had the knife. Hallie's heart was racing. "Now in my stocking. Slip it in my stocking. Hurry." The knife was cold against Hallie's leg.

"Good girl," Helga told her sister. "Rush. Go, back to the bed, sweetie."

"Papa?" Kurin was sobbing.

"He'll be okay," Hallie promised, and she felt a strength grow inside herself with the pledge.

The soles of Kurin's shoes were still visible in the doorway leading to the bedroom when the steps sounded on the porch, but she was out of sight when the door swung open.

Gid came towards Hallie. When his hands closed over her shoulders, she closed her eyes. Then she was being lifted up and thrown over his shoulder.

"We just leaving the other one?" Elton asked.

"Take her iffen you want." Gid was walking out the door.

"Naw," said Roscoe.

"Hallie . . . " Helga's words were cut off by a slap from Elton.

"Bring them dish towels for gags," Gid called back to the other men.

She was gagged before being thrown into the wagon. Johnny and Mr. Heiden, at the other end, also had their mouths covered. Hallie was able to scoot around on her side to see them in the moonlight. There was blood on Johnny's cheek and lips, but it was too dark to see exactly where the injury was.

Her body ached from the rough fall into the wagon, but it was only her leg that Hallie thought of. Against it she could still feel the knife. Elton hadn't done a good job on her hands. If she could loosen the knot . . . She began to strain, pushing to undo the rope that tied her. There was some give. Still, even if she got free, what could one girl with a knife do against three men with guns? She bit hard into her lip. Don't give up, she told herself. You can't give up now.

Her hands pressed against the strands even after she could feel the blood on her skin.

So intent was Hallie that she was almost unaware of Elton and Roscoe as they tied their horses behind the wagon before climbing to the seat.

Gid was mounting his horse when her attention was jerked momentarily away from the ropes. "What you aiming to do to the girl?" Elton wanted to know.

"It ain't smart to take her into town. Folks won't take to seeing no girl roughed up."

"I want her to see the hanging." Gid's voice was slurred by alcohol.

"Elton's right," said Roscoe. "That ain't the thing to do."

"Leave her be for now, then," Gid snapped. "I'll just have to watch for a place near town to stash her for later."

Hallie worked her bloody wrists hard against the rope. If she and Gid were alone when he hid her, if only the wagon would go on, leaving her alone with Gid. He might turn his back. It seemed long ago that she had wondered about her ability to use the knife on anyone. When she had done what had to be done, she would take Gid's horse and ride for help. Where? She would go to Pa. Her father would help her because he would have to. She would go to Pa and the boys. Somehow, somehow they would stop the hanging. The binding around Hallie's wrist gave a little, and she worked on. Hope made her strong.

At last the rope was loose enough to slip her hands out, but instead she left the rope in place and bent to loosen the one around her legs. She had to look tied, and yet she had to be ready. She wondered if Johnny and Mr. Heiden could see what she was doing, but she doubted if they could. The moon had gone behind a cloud leaving the wagon darker now.

Gid had been riding ahead, but Hallie heard his horse coming back to the wagon. "Pull over," he said. "Think I'll just take the girl out and have it over with her now."

"Why not? You can catch up to us iffen it don't take too long." Elton laughed, and the wagon stopped moving.

Soon, thought Hallie. Soon. But she lay very still. Gid was in the wagon lifting her now to the edge. He'll throw me, she thought, but her only concern was for the knife. It had to stay in her stocking. It had to. She felt it there during the moment of freedom as she flew over the wagon's side.

She was beside the road watching the wagon wheel begin to move, and Gid was standing over her. She could still hear the rattle of rocks as the others moved away. Be careful, she told herself, wait till Elton and Roscoe are gone.

"We're about to finish what we done started once, girlie." Gid's voice was low and horrible.

Yes, thought Hallie, about to finish. She moved her leg to feel the knife.

When he turned to tie his horse, she pulled and kicked with one swift motion and was up. The moon was out again. Gid's back was before her, waiting. With the knife above her head, she ran toward him.

"What the devil?" He moved, but still she slashed out, and a line of blood was visible on his shirtsleeve. "You cut me, girlie." His eyes narrowed, and he leaned menacingly toward Hallie, who was half crouching before him.

"Cut you, did I? I'll kill you, you black bastard." Again she leaped toward him. This time Gid backed off quickly, and he cursed as he stumbled.

At once Hallie was kneeling over him, and she saw the fear in his eyes. It made her feel stronger. She was full of the night air and the mountains were pushing inside her chest.

She raised the knife higher, ready to plunge into his chest, but she stopped. He was a human being. Was there another way? But suddenly a huge hand closed over her wrist.

"Don't want no one cut up on this road. Folks sure to be blaming me." It was Harp Otis, and he pulled Hallie to her feet.

"He tried to hurt me," Hallie pleaded. "Please help me."

Harp reached for the gun leaning against his leg. "Ain't nobody hurting nobody on this road."

Gid jumped to his feet. He was all sweetness. "No sirree,

no use for bloodshed." He laughed. "You know how it is, spooning gets out of hand sometimes."

"Liar." Hallie pulled at Harp's sleeve. "Did you see that wagon? They're on their way to town, going to hang innocent men."

Harp shrugged. "Don't care what they do in town. This road's all concerns me."

"Won't be no more trouble." Gid was inching toward his horse. Hallie opened her mouth to protest, but he was on the animal now, and urging it into a run.

"Stop," thundered Harp. "Didn't say you could go. Now you got me mad." He raised his gun, aimed, and fired. The bullet swished through the air, but it flew past Gid's head. "Damn it. Missed. Can't see no good at night." Ignoring Hallie, he turned and began to walk away.

"Wait," she ran after him. "Won't you help me? Please take me to town. Oh, please, Mr. Otis. Take me to town."

"Feather ain't made to carry two."

"Let me ride him then." She stepped in front of him, pleading. "They're about to hang two good men." She leaned close trying to see his eyes, hoping for sympathy there.

"Take Feather?" he questioned.

She folded her hands in supplication. "Please. I'm Mason Horton's girl."

"Don't know." He was rubbing his chin, but they were in front of his house. The horse stood in the yard, and Hallie ran toward it. Harp made no move to stop her.

A burst of strength came to enable her to fling her body

onto the horse's back, righting herself into riding position even as she urged him on. "Getty up, Feather," she commanded. Remembering Turner's experience, she feared he would not go away from his master and his home, but something, some force in her words must have reached the animal. They were moving quickly through the moonlight. Not looking back at Harp, Hallie bent low against Feather's neck and spurred him on with words and with her knees.

"He's smart and fast," Turner had said about Feather, and it was true, faster Hallie believed than Erwart's automobile. So even was his gait, so quick his movement that Hallie had the sensation of watching the bare trees along the roadside speeding past her. "God," she prayed. "Oh, dear God, don't let me be too late."

12

THE TOWN SEEMED BIGGER. Lights were everywhere, and the stirring people forced Hallie to pull back on Feather's bridle. Groups of women and children huddled together on the edge of yards, but the real crowd was at the big rock schoolhouse. No need to fasten Feather. He would go immediately home. Jumping from his back, Hallie gathered her skirt and landed running.

No one stepped aside for her, but she elbowed her way through. "We ain't had a hanging in town for fifteen year," a tall man was saying as she pushed between him and his listener, but she did not pause to look at either of them.

But at the front she stopped suddenly to stare up toward the top of the great lantern-lit steps. There against the rock building wall were Johnny and Mr. Heiden, bound and gagged. Gid was beside them with Elton and Roscoe. Dad Henderson sat on the first step, leaning against the rail.

Think, she told herself. Come up with a plan. Gid was talking. "I been over there." He was making an effort not to slur his words. "Over there fighting for my country, getting myself burned up while this here no-good were hiding." He gave Johnny a vicious poke in the ribs with his gun. There was no time to think. With a deep breath she put her foot on the first step. Johnny was looking at her, and the message in his eyes gave her courage to shove between him and Gid. "Not hiding," she shouted to the crowd, and she searched their faces, hoping to see someone, anyone, to help.

The judge! Talk to him, she thought. Whirling to the old man on the steps she added, "Johnny Childers was fixing to turn hisself in. He's hurt. They don't hang injured men. Kurt Heiden was just being kind. He didn't do nothing wrong."

"Huh?" Dad put his cupped hand to his ear. "What's that about a song?"

"Give the go-ahead, Dad," Gid urged more loudly. "Say the word and we'll sling him up." Hallie's glance followed Gid's pointing finger to the huge oak tree on the left. Two stark ropes dangled from its bare branches.

"Wait," she screamed, her eyes falling on Preacher De-Witt and his wife. "Preacher," she cried. "You won't let them do this? It ain't right. You know it ain't right." An idea came to her. "Remember the Christmas trees? Remember how Mr. Heiden always brung the trees for the Christmas doings? The prettiest trees. You going to hang him now?" She addressed the man's wife. "Mrs. DeWitt, you recollect my brother. He's in the army now. Don't you know how he stood up for Mr. Heiden?"

Someone was pushing through the crowd. Ruby! Ruby was coming to stand beside her. Hallie felt stronger. "Listen to Hallie," Ruby shouted as she climbed the steps.

There were murmurs in the group, but Hallie heard one voice clearly. "She's right," a small woman at the front pulled on her husband's arm, but he ignored her.

Hallie wiped at her face with the palms of her hands. Think, she told herself. You've got to think. Think of something good.

Female images stood out from the crowd. Then her eyes fell on Mrs. Atkins. Mrs. Atkins who had marched in a women's rights parade. "Mrs. Atkins," she called, "you know us womenfolk have to stand up. Even President Wilson says we will have the vote soon, and it's time we had our say in this town."

She pointed to Gid. "This man tried to have his way with me last summer. Pinned down my arms and slapped my face. Likely would have killed me if Johnny Childers hadn't stopped him." Her voice seemed to echo out among the faces, and they quieted. "Johnny's not a bad man." Hallie stepped back to put her hands on his shoulders. "He just hates this war, would rather go to jail than to fight. Is that so wrong, to dread killing and being shot at?"

She put out her other hand to indicate Kurt Heiden. "Here is a man cared for his daughters his ownself, all gentle like. You seen him helping his neighbors. We going to kill him here in Lafine because of where he was born? Is that the kind of town we want? We got to stand up and stop the hating." She held out her arms to them. "Come join me, modern women. Come make your voices heard."

Exhausted, she moved to lean against the top of the rail,

but her eyes never left the women of the crowd. And they were moving. Stepping away from their menfolk, they were coming. First Mrs. Atkins in her patent leather shoes, and then others. Up the stairs to stand beside her, they came. Mrs. DeWitt came and even Mrs. Tanner. Women whom Hallie did not know came, some with babies in their arms, one old one leaning on a walking stick.

There was no need to lean now. Hallie's body straightened, and joy was in her shout. "No hanging," she declared, and they joined her chant. "No hanging," as they lined the steps.

"Dad!" Gid was frantic and moved close to the old man's face. "You fixing to listen to a bunch of women, or you going to pay heed to an injured soldier?" He rubbed his hand slowly across his red scarred face, and opened his mouth to say more, only to be drowned out by a great voice.

Mary was working her way through to the steps. "Ain't but one person I know has broke the law." She spat off the edge of the steps. "No, that ain't exactly true. I done wrong too."

"Ma, please," protested Gid like a child, running to her.

Except for the hand that shot out to grab his collar, she paid him no mind. "I come here looking for this no-account, knowed in my soul he weren't up to no good. The blame comes to me. Fellow from the army come after him just yesterday, but I lied. Said I hadn't seen Gid." She jerked hard on the collar. "He weren't injured in no war like he claims. Fellow told me all about Gid not getting past Texas. Went pestering after some woman. It were her poured boiling water on him when he tried to ruin her." She paused to spit again. "Then he slipped off from the hospital and showed up to home." She faced her son, and he ducked his head. "I ought not to have hid him." She shook her head in disgust. "Claimed he done learnt his lesson. Me wanting to believe him, all hurt like he were." She wiped her free hand across her face.

Oscar Henderson, who acted as deputy, stepped up to take Gid, and Hallie looked around to see Elton and Roscoe jump from the edge of the steps and disappear into the darkness.

Everything was a whirl, women gathering around Hallie to squeeze her hand, Johnny and Mr. Heiden being untied. Mason and the boys, alerted by Helga and Kurin, had arrived.

"You should have come to me, daughter," he told Hallie quietly when the chance came. "Me and the boys may as well wait in the wagon," he added moving away. Then, stepping back to her, he murmured quickly, "You was right to stand up."

The tears came then, not great sobs but full tears of relief, and Hallie made no attempt to stop them. Johnny came to her, and she leaned against him unself-consciously.

People were moving, heading back to their homes, where they would rehash it all over and over. "Mr. Heiden," called Mrs. DeWitt, "will you bring the tree this year? You got such pretty pines."

"Please, Kurt," her husband added. "We'd be obliged. Been missing you in services, too." His voice was sheepish, apologetic.

The big man had an arm around each of his daughters. "*Ja*," he said. "*Ja*. We will bring the Christmas tree."

"I've got my rig," said the preacher. "We will drive you home. Tie the girls' horses behind."

Johnny, it was decided, would spend another night with the Heidens and catch the early morning train. "We have to say good-bye now," he said, and, taking Hallie's hand, he led her down the steps and away from the others.

"I never was so scared, so awful scared of what they would do to you," her voice shook.

"It's over now, and you were wonderful. I owe you my life for a second time." He pulled her to him, stroking her hair.

Then Mason was beside them. Johnny put out his hand, and Hallie was relieved to see her father shake it. "I'm Johnny Childers, sir," he said. With a glance toward the wagon full of waiting people, he went on. "I've not got long to talk, and I can see how you might have objections. Still, I'm begging permission to court your daughter when my name is cleared of trouble."

"She's young," said Mason, but he laughed. "Reckon after tonight, though, can't anybody argue she ain't a woman grown."

Hallie hoped Mason would walk away, but he stood his ground. "I'll write to you," said Johnny. He touched her cheek, and then he was gone. She held her breath as he ran toward the wagon, which soon disappeared into the night.

"Time we went home," said Mason, who had stood quietly beside her as she watched. Hallie was asleep on the wagon floor even before they were out of Lafine, and her pa helped her into the house as if she were Dovie.

In the early morning stillness of the next day, Hallie heard the train whistle. It was rare for the sound to carry over the mountains in the daytime. It's a good-bye, she thought. It's a good-bye from Johnny Childers.

When the letter came from Johnny's aunt, it was full of gratitude. Johnny, she said, was in jail, but she had real hope. There were plans for Hallie's schooling and money for her trip.

Mason accepted that Hallie would go. "The world's changing," he declared as if the whole thing had been his idea. "A woman's got to learn nowadays same as a man."

A letter also came from Johnny. "Aunt Abby's got me an excellent lawyer," he wrote, "but even better, she's got all her women friends taking up for me." Hallie could imagine his smile as he had written, "I've seen what women can do." At the end of the letter he added, "I've just about decided to study medicine if I get out of this all right. I'd like to use my hands for healing. How would you feel about someday being a doctor's wife?"

For a long time she sat still under the pine tree where she had gone to be alone for the reading, and she studied the mountain side, longing for sight of Johnny's absent campfire.

When she rose it was to climb higher up the hill. There, near a patch of vines that would bear huckleberries in the spring, she found Star's rock. Years earlier, he had scratched his name, big and straight, in the limestone. Dropping beside the moss-covered boulder, Hallie leaned against it. "Star," she said aloud, "so much is changing for me, and you not here." Carefully, she traced the letters of his name. Then, humming softly, she made her way home.

Back at the cabin, visitors waited. Hallie was greeted by Vida Mae, eager to discuss the job. Her mother, who accompanied her, was also eager. "Man alone like that. Why, we'd just be tickled to help, don't you know," the woman told Hallie.

There was renewed ambition in Mrs. Willbanks's voice, and Hallie smiled. Reporting on the pursuit of their father would give the boys something to fill letters.

Hallie brought baby Pearly to the cabin. She spent her last few days there rocking him by the fire, cleaning, and preparing the young ones for her departure. "I'll be home for Christmas," she assured them. "We'll go to the doings in town, and I'll bring presents."

On the Tuesday of her departure, she was up early. Many of the farewells had been said—Helga, Ruby, who was now Mrs. Tanner. Even Mary had come with little Woodrow to say good-bye. There was only the cabin, the family, and the hills to be parted from.

The girl moved about the only home she had ever known, touching objects in Ma's kitchen and the Grimm fairy tale book she was leaving for Dovie.

It was Mason who came last to say good-bye. He kept his distance and would have backed away after the muttered farewell, but Hallie stopped him. I'm not the same, she marveled, not like I used to be. With wonder and joy she found herself crying in his arms.

"Shush, now," he said softly. "It's right, you going."

Brack was already waiting in the wagon when she stopped at her mother's rosebush. One red flower, the last survivor, hung on tenaciously. Summer was only a memory. The rose would fall soon. Removal took only a slight pull.

"Will you put it on your dress?" asked Dovie.

"It's not strong enough. All the petals would fall off." Hallie touched the flower to the little girl's cheek. "I'll press it in the pages of one of my new books." She held the flower, carefully protecting it during the good-bye hugs.

Brack sat quietly with the reins. "I can't say no more good-byes," he had warned her when it was arranged that he would drive her to the train.

Neither did Hallie want to talk. There was memory work to be done. With each turn of the wagon wheels, she studied the trees, the rocks, the glimpses of the creek alongside the trail.

But when they came to Lafine, good-byes were forgotten. Even at the edge of town it was plain that something unusual was happening. People were moving about, obviously celebrating.

Preacher DeWitt stood on the depot steps. "Praise God," he shouted, and hats went flying into the air.

Brack stopped the horses and stood up. "What is it?" he called.

"Armistice," someone yelled. "War's over!"

"Yippee!" Brack was on the ground, tossing his hat into the air.

Hallie's hand flew to her head, but she was hatless. There was nothing, nothing but the flower. Climbing to stand on the wagon seat, she wound up her arm and hurled the rose high, toward the sun.